ALSO BY Donna Schwartze

Eight Years (The Trident Trilogy: Book One)
Wild Card (The Trident Trilogy: Book Three)

The Only Reason is the second book of The Trident Trilogy.
Buy the other two books, *Eight Years* and *Wild Card*, on
Amazon.

THE ONLY REASON
(THE TRIDENT TRILOGY: BOOK TWO)

DONNA SCHWARTZE

Copyright © 2020 by Donna Schwartze

ISBN: 9798562490162

Published by Donna Schwartze, 2020

donnaschwartzeauthor@gmail.com

❀ Created with Vellum

THE ONLY REASON

(The Trident Trilogy: Book Two)

DONNA SCHWARTZE

For my mom, who taught me the importance of independence and showed me the true power of strength.

"I am not to speak to you,
I am to think of you when I sit alone
or wake at night alone,
I am to wait,
I do not doubt I am to meet you again,
I am to see to it that I do not lose you."

—Walt Whitman, "To a Stranger"

Prologue

As he climbed down into the dimly lit tunnel, he heard the house explode above him. He instinctively flung his body to the ground and covered his head. The tunnel walls shook violently, but didn't collapse.

He quickly got to his feet and flipped his goggles down to help see through the wall of dust ahead of him. As the tunnel began to clear, he started running. It only took a few minutes for their screaming voices to fade out behind him.

Chapter One

"Damn, Mills," Mack said as Millie cut back over the top of the soft wave she was riding and glided perfectly into place next to his board. "You're getting almost as good as me."

Millie plopped down on her board next to him. "Almost? C'mon, Dad. You know I've been better than you for quite a while now."

"Okay," Mack said, laughing. "Someone's getting a little too cocky about her skills."

"You know what you always tell me: 'It's not bragging if it's true.' And I think we both know it's true." She tilted her head and smiled angelically at him.

Mack slapped his huge hand in the water, sending a tidal wave crashing into Millie's face.

"Dad! So rude!" Millie tried to return the favor, but Mack quickly grabbed both of her wrists and pulled her board closer to him.

"You will never be faster than me, grasshopper. Never," he said as she fruitlessly tried to break his hold. "Do you give?"

She snarled playfully at him. "Fine. You're faster than me. Just not on a surfboard."

"Milllllllllieeeee!" They turned to see a boy from her high school paddling quickly over to them.

"Hey, Jake," Millie said, leaning forward to give him a fist bump as he floated up to her.

"I saw your last ride," Jake said. "Totally crushed it as usual."

Millie looked right at Mack and grinned. "Thanks, Jake. I've always said you're a great judge of surfing skill."

"For sure." Jake sat up on his board and gestured to Mack. "He's a little old for you, don't you think?"

"Eww! You weirdo. He's my dad," Millie said, punching Jake in the arm. "Dad, this is Jake."

"Oh man. Mr. Marsh. Sorry, dude. I don't see many dads with that much facial fur. You know?" Jake said, rubbing his hands over his own stubble.

Mack nodded, making no attempt to shake Jake's outstretched hand.

Millie laughed as she looked at Mack's face. "Uh, Jake. We're about to paddle in. I'll catch you later."

Jake looked away quickly from Mack's glaring eyes. "Yeah. Cool, Mill. Have a good ride."

As Jake paddled away, Millie looked back at Mack. "Dad. We're not dating. He's just a friend."

Mack sighed and looked up at the sky. "Do you remember when you were little and you were only friends with girls?" he said wistfully. "Those were good days."

Millie rolled her eyes. "One of these days, I'm going to meet a guy you think is good enough for me, and you're going to beg me to marry him."

Mack shook his head. "Never going to happen. Never. There's not anyone even close to good enough for you."

Millie smiled. "Ooh, Dad. Speaking of my girlfriends, did I tell you about Chloe's birthday party? It was a circus theme. And you know what that means . . ."

"Clowns," Mack said, shuddering.

"Yep. They were all over the place. As much as you hate clowns, you wouldn't have lasted two seconds at this party."

"Millie. They're clowns. Everyone should hate them. They're diabolical and evil. I still can't understand how I raised a daughter who likes clowns."

"How is it that you can hunt down terrorists every day on your job and not be scared at all? But you see a big red nose and floppy shoes and you're terrified?"

"It's simple—I can shoot the terrorists. I can't shoot the clowns," Mack said. "If I'm ever able to shoot the clowns, it will be a game changer."

"I don't think that's going to happen, Dad."

"Mills, are you sure you don't want a big sweet sixteen party like Chloe's? Without the clowns, of course."

"My birthday was in January."

"It's not too late. The entire year is your sixteenth year. Maybe we can have a party before we go to San Diego in a couple weeks."

"I still don't want a party, Dad. All I want for any birthday is to spend time with you," Millie said, reaching over to hold his hand. "That and the car you bought me, of course."

"Of course," Mack said, smiling. "It's not much of a car, but it gets you out of the house and away from Camille until we move this fall. That's another thing. Are you completely sure you don't want to do your senior year of high school here? I don't mind living in the Outer Banks while you finish. We don't have to live with Camille. We can rent a place until you graduate, and then move."

"Seriously, Dad. I just want to be with you. And I think a fresh start would be the best for us. You know? I want to move to San Diego as soon as we can. I don't mind finishing high school out there. It's more about my time with you."

Mack nodded. "Well, I don't officially retire until September, so if you change your mind, it's fine. We'll work it out."

"I won't change my mind. I have our move date as September 24. That's what's happening."

"Okay, princess. As you wish. We'll go out there the first weekend of August and start looking for a house. We can enroll you in school when we find one."

"Will you please, please, please reconsider letting me get my GED and starting UCSD early? I talked to them, and they said I have enough college credits already to get accepted into their oceanography program."

Mack took a deep breath. "I know, sweetie, but you're already so young for your grade. And I thought you hated science."

"I don't hate it. I just think it's boring in high school. If it's about the ocean, I will love it. I want to be an ocean conservationist."

"You would be great at that. You'll be amazing at whatever you want to do. Maybe finish high school and try not to be in such a rush about everything. We've got nothing but time ahead of us."

"Okay. But you know if I'm in college, we can go surfing between my classes," Millie said as her eyes started to sparkle mischievously. "And we both know you need as much practice as you can get if you're going to keep up with me on those breaks in the Pacific."

Mack shook his head, trying not to smile. "You know San Diego is where I did my SEAL training. I know that ocean really well. Any home-field advantage you think you have here is going to be completely wiped away when we get out there. I will be the dominant surfer again."

"Again?" Millie said. "So you're admitting you're not the dominant surfer now."

Mack lunged forward quickly, tackling Millie off her board and plunging them both into the water. The ocean swallowed up Millie's peal of laughter as they went under. Mack surfaced first and pushed their surfboards out of the way as he pulled her up.

"I will always be the king of the sea," he said as he lifted her under her arms and tossed her a couple feet away from him.

Millie giggled. "Okay, Poseidon. You win."

Mack reached for her hand and pulled her back to him. "Let's make a deal. We'll get out to San Diego in September and chill until the end of the year. You can start school in January at wherever we decide together is the right place."

Millie put up her hands for a double high-five. "Deal," she

said as she slapped his hands. "I can't wait to chill with you—with only you. It sounds like pure heaven."

"How many days until it happens?"

"The board in my bedroom says seventy days." Millie started her countdown calendar a year before they were scheduled to move. Three hundred and sixty-five days had slowly—excruciatingly so for Millie—become seventy. She couldn't believe they only had a little over two months until it happened.

"I can't wait until it gets here." Mack kissed her forehead before he helped her back on her board. "Are you done surfing? I'm starving. Maybe we can go to that new burger place."

"Ooh. Yeah. And it's right next to the ice cream shop. Let's go there for dessert. Their strawberry ice cream is amazing," Millie said as she started lining up her board. "That's my favorite flavor."

"I know it is, sweetie," Mack said, smiling as he got back on his own board. "It's all you've eaten since you were a baby."

He sighed as she paddled into her last wave of the day. Sometimes his heart physically ached when he watched her. This was one of those times. He would do anything to keep her safe and happy. He couldn't believe the time was coming where they would get to see each other every day. He waited sixteen years for this day to arrive, and it was almost here.

Now if I can just get through the next few months without getting killed, he thought as he popped up on his board and rode the next wave into shore.

Chapter Two

MILLIE, SAN DIEGO, CALIFORNIA, 2020

"Have you told him you love him yet?" Mariel peers at me over her wine glass as she takes a long, slow sip. Her expression suggests the correct answer is definitely no.

"Yes, I have," I say, draining the last of my martini to prepare for the tongue-lashing I know I'm about to receive.

"Oh my God, Millie. Why? You've only been together—really together—for two months." She shakes her head with so much force that her dangling earrings slap her repeatedly in the face.

"I said it because it's true. I do love him," I say, quickly adding, "and Mason said it, too. We're in love. Why is that bad?"

Mariel has become my best girlfriend since I moved to San Diego six months ago. Let me emphasize "girlfriend" because her husband, Chase, is my best friend. He has been since the day my dad—his best friend—died. I haven't always made it easy for Chase to love me, but he never gave up, and that's made me almost as devoted to him as I was to my dad.

Mariel motions to the waiter to bring her another glass of wine. It's her third. She usually stops at two. This is obviously about to get serious. "It's not bad, Millie. It's just unrealistic. You aren't living in the real world right now. You're still recovering from the kidnapping. He's still adjusting from stepping down as an active SEAL. You both had traumatic, life-changing things happen recently. You shouldn't be making big decisions."

"I don't think being in love is a decision. It just kind of happens."

She rests her chin on her hands as she bats her eyelashes. "Oh, sweetie. That entire statement makes me want to slap you so badly."

"What? How long did it take you to realize you were in love with Chase?"

"I'll let you know when it happens." She flashes her most wicked smile at me.

"Mariel!"

I've known them since I was sixteen. They took me in for a few months after my dad died. They have the most loving marriage I've ever seen, but they are complete opposites. Deep down, Chase—like me—is a dreamer. Mariel is not. She's 100 percent pragmatic all the time. It's probably why Chase married her. It's definitely why I value her friendship. She keeps us grounded.

"Of course I love him, Millie. But it hasn't always been easy. It took Chase years to adjust to not being active anymore. I'm still not sure he's there, and it's been almost ten years. Our marriage has taken a lot of work. A lot. I'm just saying this little blissful bubble you and Mason are in right now isn't going to last."

The waiter thankfully delivers me another martini. "Well even if reality sets in—"

Before I can finish, Mariel grabs my hand across the table and pats it. "Not if, sweetie. When. When it sets in."

"When," I say sharply. "When it sets in, I'm still going to love him."

She sits back and crosses her arms. We stare at each other for a few minutes before she finally says, "And what are you going to say when he asks you to marry him?"

I roll my eyes so severely, it almost gives me a headache. "Oh my God, Mar. He's not going to ask me to marry him. You're drunk."

"I am." She smiles. "But that doesn't mean I'm wrong. That's what comes after the 'I love you': marriage then babies. And I know you're not ready for all that. Are you?"

"No. God, no. Not even close." I'm starting to think the double shot in my second martini was a mistake. My brain's getting fuzzy. "He's not either. I know that. I mean it's only been two months."

She flings her hands in the air like she's suddenly conducting an orchestra. "And finally you say something that makes sense," she says, slamming her hands back down on the table. She hits them five more times to emphasize each of her next words. "It's only been two months."

"I really hate you right now." I eat the last olive from my martini and fling the cocktail pick at her.

She laughs victoriously. "Have you even had a fight with

him yet? Do you know enough about each other to disagree on anything?"

"There is one thing we argue about," I say slowly.

"Ooh. Do tell."

"Well, you know how independent I am—"

"Girl, please." She starts massaging her temples. "I almost killed you during your college years. You put us through hell with your bullshit independence."

"I'm not explaining my reasons for that again," I say, pointing at her. "Let's stay focused on the present, please."

"Fine. Please go on, princess." She drains the last of her third glass of wine.

"Well, we've been having arguments because Mason is overly protective of me, and it's driving me a little crazy. For some reason, he feels responsible for my kidnapping—even though he wasn't there. It's made him start acting like my bodyguard as much as he acts like my boyfriend. He tries to control everything. And I've never been very good at being controlled."

She takes a deep breath. "Yeah. That's something Chase and I went through. First, you know that's just part of who they are. That's what they do for a living—SEALs protect people. They control people. It's hard for them to do that at work and then completely turn it off when they get home. It took years for Chase to turn that down and he's not nearly as alpha as Mason. You probably need to give him a break. But bottom line, he's never going to lose that completely. So you either learn how to live with it or the relationship isn't going to work."

That's not the advice I wanted. I was hoping she would

have a magic solution—like a pill Mason could take to turn down the alpha a little bit.

"And second," she continues, "the reason he feels responsible for the kidnapping is precisely because he wasn't there. He and his team worked the mission with you from day one. Then not to be there when the shit really went down—that's a tough pill for these guys to swallow. Add in the way he feels about you, and I'm sure it's enough to make his head feel like it's going to explode. He thinks he failed you and failed at the mission. These guys don't like to fail and they rarely do. It's tough on them."

"So what you're telling me is that I'm the problem. That I need to let him control me because of the way he's programmed."

"I'm saying because of the way he's programmed, he's going to control things one way or another. Whether you can tolerate it is up to you. Do you think you can give him a little control here and there?"

"Yeah. I mean, I do already. There are areas where I don't mind it at all."

"Sexually." She nods her head way too enthusiastically.

"Oh my God! I didn't say that."

"But the sex is great, right? You know what I'm saying. When they get all alpha and take control—"

"Mar! You're like my mom. Stop it." I bury my face in my hands and then peer through my fingers at her. "But yeah. It's out of this world. Like crazy good."

She makes a check mark in the air with her finger. "Knew it," she says smugly. "And that's part of what's blinding you from reality. No judgment on that part though. Get yours, you know?"

"Oh my God. No more wine for you. You're out of control."

She stands up suddenly, swaying slightly. "I'm going to the bathroom. It will give you ample time to think about how right I am about everything."

I watch her until the click of her stilettos fades away into the restaurant. I know she's right about the blissful bubble. Since Mason moved here, we've survived on a steady diet of sex and surfing—absolutely no real-world problems allowed. It's been breathtaking. But in the last few weeks, a few ugly issues have been trying to creep into our utopia.

Captain Culver—Mason's old boss—called him last week and asked him to take control of his SEAL team again. The guy who replaced him was injured and won't be back for months. Mason said no, but I can tell he wanted to say yes. He misses that life. It's something I don't understand—that absolute love for your job. My dad felt that way about the teams, too. He told me he thought about quitting every day after I was born. He never did, though. And sixteen years later, he died on the job. I can't take another man I love dying that way. Mason knows that, but it doesn't make him miss the job any less.

My old boss, George, has been calling me, too. He wants me to come back to the CIA. I have absolutely no interest in going back. I chose that career path only to find out who my mom was and who killed her. I spent eight years focused on almost nothing else. I know the truth now. I have no need to be at the agency anymore. And, more importantly, I have no desire to be there. My biggest problem is that I have no idea what I want to do with my life now.

Mason's regretting his decision. I can't make a decision. It's all threatening the bubble. I hate when Mariel is right. But it looks like reality might be starting to set in. All I want to do right now is go home and cuddle up on the couch with Mason —maybe keep the bubble intact for at least one more night.

Chapter Three

"Well look who decided to join us," Jack says as I grab a beer from the cooler. "Did Millie give you permission to leave the house tonight?"

I scoop a handful of ice out of the cooler and dump it down his shirt. He jumps up like someone set off a bottle rocket under his chair. I walk around the fire-pit and take the chair next to Chase.

Since I moved to San Diego a couple months ago, I've been adopted into the weekly gathering of retired SEALs. Jack —the oldest of us all—hosts whomever shows up every Wednesday night on his back patio. When a bunch of old operators get together, there's a lot of beer and stories about our time in service. Most of these guys have been out ten years or more. I've only been away from my team for two months. I'm not quite ready to talk about it like it's in the past.

That's one of the reasons I rarely show up, but for probably the first time in his life, Jack's actually right about something. My main reason is that I want to be with Millie as much as possible. Being away from her when I'm at the base is torture. When I'm done with work, I go straight to her house. If she didn't go out with her friends every once in a while, I don't think I'd ever be away from her. Tonight, she's out with Chase's wife, Mariel.

"You heard from the ladies yet?" Chase says, shaking his head. "The last time they went out together, they ended up in the ocean fully clothed."

"Yeah, I remember. Millie shook for an hour even after she dried off and buried herself in a mound of blankets." I smile as I think about the five or six blankets that always clutter her bed. I still haven't figured out how someone can be so cold all the time when it's almost always seventy degrees here.

"I told Mar to try to stick to two glasses of wine tonight, but no promises. She gets cranked up when she's around Millie."

Jack has finally cleared the ice out of his shirt. He plops back down in his chair and clears his throat loudly to make sure everyone's paying attention to him again. He's one of those guys who never knows when to quit.

"I'm just saying the sex has to be out of this world to have the great Mason Davis all whipped up like this," he says, peering at me over his glasses as he stokes the fire-pit with an old broom handle.

"Worry more about your own sex life. Or lack of one," I say as my empty beer can lands perfectly in the middle of his forehead.

"He's not wrong, Jack. When's the last time you even

touched a woman?" Chase drains the last of his beer and heads over to the cooler for another.

"Damn. If I had someone who looked like Millie, I wouldn't be able to walk straight." Jack just can't stop himself. His voice is getting a little shaky. He knows he's about to step on a land mine, but he keeps going. "The last time I saw her—at Charlie's—she was wearing that little sundress number that just barely covered—"

"Watch your mouth," I say sternly as Chase comes up behind him and almost knocks his head clear off his body with a swift backhand.

"Don't talk about her like that again," Chase says in a friendly tone, but his body language—including the finger that's inches from Jack's face—is telling a different story.

Jack tries to recover some of his swagger. "All right. All right. I know Princess Millie is off limits. I'll back off. But only for her dad. Mack was the toughest fucker I ever met. I think he could probably still kick my ass from his grave."

Chase rolls his eyes as he makes his way back over to me. "Ignore him," he says as he hands me another beer.

"I always do." I take a long swig. "Hey. Did Millie tell you about my replacement going down?"

"No, man. Just injured, I hope."

"Yeah. Nothing serious. He tore his ACL. They want me to take the team back for a few months while he recovers."

Chase raises his eyebrows. "How does Millie feel about that?"

"After the fight we had today, I'm guessing she's all in favor of it."

"What was the fight about? Same thing?"

"Yeah. You know how she is. She's defiant about me trying to protect her. She's so damn stubborn about it. I'm really trying to back off, but with everything that's happened to her in the last year, it's not easy to be laid-back about it, you know?"

"You don't need to tell me about Millie's stubborn streak. That child almost gave me a heart attack during her college years. I've told you what she put us through. I felt like I was tracking a fugitive."

I shake my head. "Her old agency boss has been calling her, too. He wants her back in D.C. I don't think she really has much interest in it."

"From what she's told me, she doesn't have any interest in it. Do you want to go back to active duty? Or do you feel like you're done with that life?"

"You've been gone for, what, about ten years? Do you feel like you're done?"

Chase takes a long drink. "No, man. I would still do it today if my body would let me. It never really leaves you, does it?"

"I miss it every day. Training the new guys out on Coronado is fine. It's something to do with my day, but it's nothing like being on a mission—leading your team. You know. You were a team leader a lot longer than I was."

"Yeah. Obviously at my age, I can't go back, but you still have a few years if you want to do it. You think that might be part of the problem with you and Millie? Maybe you're regretting leaving your team and moving out here."

"No, I don't regret it. She's the only reason I'm here, but it was the right decision. If Culver hadn't called, I wouldn't even be thinking about it. You think he did it on purpose? He's never really been a fan of Millie and me being together."

Chase laughs loudly. "You think he's assigning team leads to break up a relationship? Get it together, man. You're losing it. Harry's not like that. You know how buttoned up he is. Even when he was a grunt on my team, he was always the most serious one in the group. He asked you because that's your team. You could slip back in without missing a beat."

"Yeah, I know. My mind's mush right now. Maybe it's this California air or something," I say, sighing loudly. "And I haven't had a decent night's sleep in a few days."

"Man, if it's because y'all are having too much sex or something, please keep that to yourself."

"You are the last person I want to talk to about my sex life with Millie—the absolute last."

"Appreciate that, brother," he says as he slugs me on the shoulder. "So why aren't you sleeping? PTSD? Nightmares?"

"Yeah, but not mine. Millie's starting to have nightmares."

"Starting? You mean about Mack? She's been having those since the day she found out he was dead," Chase says quietly. "The first night she stayed with Mar and me, she woke up screaming bloody murder. Scared the hell out of us. She told me they'd started to get better after you moved here. Not true?"

"Ah, man. I didn't know she'd been having them for that long. She didn't tell me. She's had a handful since I moved here. Is that better?"

"She used to have them every night so, yeah, that's better." Chase lets out a long sigh. "The ninth anniversary of his death is coming up in a few months. That's probably why they're back. I can tell she's struggling right now."

"What do you mean 'struggling'? She seems happy. She says she is."

"Look, I'm trying to stay out of your relationship, but there's probably a lot you don't know. I'm not sure how much she talks about her childhood." Chase looks away and tips his chair back as far as he can without falling over backward. "The badass-super-agent you met six months ago has maybe been around for like three or four years. Before that—especially when Mack was still alive—she was a sweet little ray of sunshine without a care in the world. Mack protected her from harsh reality—any reality. Period."

"She seems like that most of the time now—like sunny and happy. Maybe she's going back to how she was before he died. You know? Maybe finally finding out who her mom was and putting her Bosnian family behind her has freed her up."

"Yeah, I don't know. You spend a lot more time with her now than I do. But when she first moved here—when you were still on deployment—it's like there were a bunch of different Millies battling for control. I don't think she knows who she is anymore, and I can tell that's bothering her. But she'll figure it out, and I'm sure your being here is helping her do that."

Before I can answer, Chase's phone rings. He looks at me and shakes his head. "It's Mariel. Any bets on what Lucy and Ethel are up to tonight?"

"Hi, honey. Everything okay?" he says like he's talking to a first grader. "Yeah. That's a good decision. It sounds like you shouldn't drive. Mason and I are wrapping up here. We'll come and get you. Umm. George's in La Jolla? Okay. It's going to take us at least twenty minutes to get there. Promise me you won't go in the ocean. Yeah, I know. That was just that one time. Okay. Don't leave until we get there. And maybe don't have any more to drink. Okay, babe. We'll be there soon."

"Guess she had that third glass of wine, huh?" I laugh as I dump the rest of my beer in the fire and grab the car keys out of my pocket.

Chapter Four

"You got your eyes on that one, or is she still in play?" Harry said as he sat down next to Mack at the bar. He slid his glass to the bartender for a refill.

Mack's eyes were locked on the brunette sitting at the opposite side of the bar. She was talking to her friend—nervously laughing and trying desperately to act like she wasn't looking back at him. "You can try, but she's already set her sights on the gold medal. Not sure she's going to settle for the bronze at this point," Mack said as he tried to smooth his beard out a bit.

"God. I can't wait for you to move to San Diego," Harry said, shaking his head. "Maybe then there will be some left for the rest of us."

"I wouldn't count on it, brother," Mack said as he slid off his bar stool. "Now sit back and watch the master work."

The brunette watched anxiously as Mack sauntered over

and sat down next to her. She giggled as she turned to him. "My friend wants to know if you're a SEAL."

"Does she?" Mack said, putting his hand on her knee. "And what do you want to know?"

She looked down at his hand slowly and then back up at his intense stare. "Umm. I mean, I guess the same thing," she said, starting to breathe a little more heavily.

"Is that really all you want to know about me? There are so many things that are more interesting."

"Like what?" she said as her eyes widened.

"Like," Mack said as he slid forward on his stool, so their knees were almost touching, "that I make the best pancakes in the world."

She tilted her head. "It's a little late for pancakes. Don't you think?"

"Then I guess we'll just have to eat them when we wake up in the morning." Mack smiled at her as he stood up. He touched her shoulder lightly as he walked by her. "I'll be in the black truck to your right as you walk out if you want to join me."

Mack knew the women in this bar weren't much of a challenge. That amount of effort worked at least 90 percent of the time, but he had never seen this woman before. He was giving it about a seventy-thirty chance she'd show up.

He was barely in the truck when he saw her walk out of the bar and look immediately to her right. He got out and walked around to the passenger's side. He opened the door and leaned against it as he watched her walk over to him.

"Hey," she said, looking up at him.

He reached out and took her hands. "Hey."

"My friend said I can't leave with you."

"Okay. Thanks for coming out to tell me," he said, squeezing her hands lightly before he dropped them.

"Wait," she said, pressing her hands against his chest. "She said I couldn't leave with you, but I'm sure we can get creative."

"I'm very creative," he said as he spun her around and pressed her against the door. As he started kissing her, she wound her arms around his neck and buried her hands in his thick hair. He pulled up her skirt as he picked her up and sat her down on the truck seat—spreading her legs with his hips as his body pressed against her.

"Is anyone going to see us?" she whispered as she started to pull off Mack's T-shirt.

"No, baby. We're hidden over here in the corner," he growled into her ear as his hand started moving between her legs. She let out a soft moan.

He grabbed a condom out of the glove compartment and ripped it open with his teeth. He put it on with one hand as he plunged his fingers inside her with his other hand. She moaned more loudly.

"You like that? You're really going to like this," he said as he slid himself inside her. She wrapped her legs around his waist to pull him in deeper. As he rocked her back and forth against the seat, she grabbed his face and started aggressively kissing him—stopping only to let out a few more moans. She rubbed her hands through his hair again as her body shuddered against him. Mack buried his face in her shoulder as he came. He kissed her gently a few more times before he pulled out.

She stood up and pulled her skirt back down. "You are a SEAL, right?'

"Yeah." He smiled as he pulled his pants up. "I am."

She smiled broadly. "Okay. Well, I'm going to go back inside to my friends. I'll see you in there, okay?"

"Sounds good." Mack nodded as she walked around the truck. He gave her a few minutes' head start and then followed her inside.

Mack grabbed a beer at the bar before he walked over to where Chase was sitting.

"I don't know how you're going to keep whoring around like this when Millie moves in with you," Chase said.

"Ah, no. It's all done when we move. It's just me and her. No women allowed," Mack said as he pulled up a chair. "After Millie graduates from college, I might even find a nice girl like Mariel and settle down."

"First of all, you know damn well Mariel isn't a nice girl," Chase said, laughing. "And second, you think you're going to be celibate for four years?"

"Well, maybe not that long, but I can be for a while. I just want to enjoy my time with Millie. No distractions."

"Maybe when Millie's out on a date, you can sneak in a woman or two. I wouldn't want you to lose your touch."

"I will never lose my touch," Mack laughed. "And like I'm going to let Millie date."

"Brother, I've brought two daughters through the teenage years and sent them off to college. They date. They date assholes. You're going to have to grin and bear it. Living with her all the time is going to be an eye-opener for you."

Mack sighed. "Man, I can't wait. It's going be the best

time of my life. Bring on the problems. Bring on the asshole boyfriends. I'm ready to be a full-time dad."

"Hey!" Mack and Chase looked up to see a man standing over them. He pointed at Mack. "Did you take my girlfriend outside?"

"Depends," Mack said, taking a long drink of his beer. "Who's your girlfriend?"

"Speaking of asshole boyfriends." Chase rolled his eyes as he stood up and pushed the man back away from Mack. "Believe me, brother. You don't want any part of him."

The man shook Chase's hand off and stepped toward Mack again. He pointed at the brunette across the bar. "My girlfriend is the one with the red shirt. I saw you walk in behind her."

Mack stood up slowly. The rest of his team started gathering behind him. "First of all, I didn't *take* anyone anywhere. And second, you've got about five seconds to back off."

"You need all them to fight me?" the man said, gesturing to the team.

Mack laughed, not turning around. "They're just here to watch. You want to fight? Take your best shot."

The man started walking away before he turned back suddenly and ran at Mack, trying to tackle him around the waist. Mack stepped slightly to the side and caught the man around the neck. He pushed him back roughly.

"I'll let you get away with that one, but that's the only pass you get," Mack said.

Chase walked between them, looking at the man. "Take the pass," he said, shaking his head. "Save yourself. She ain't worth it."

"Get out of my way," the man growled at Chase.

"All right, brother," Chase said, sighing. "Go get 'em."

The man squared up with Mack—his fists in front of his face—as he began to shift from foot to foot. Mack rolled his eyes and remained relaxed.

"Stay away from my girlfriend," the man growled, finally taking a very wild haymaker at Mack.

Mack easily grabbed his arm, held it high in the air, and put a quick uppercut into his ribs. The force of the blow lifted the man off the ground. Mack let go of his arm and let him fall to the floor.

"Damn, Mack. I think I heard at least two of his ribs break," Harry said from behind him.

The man rolled over, crying out as he grabbed his ribs. Mack sighed and walked away.

Chase lifted the man off the floor, putting his arm around him. He walked him to the door and patted him on the back. "You're going to want to go to the emergency room."

Mack shook his head as Chase walked back over to him. "I tried to warn him. I always give them an out."

"You can only do so much. There's no fixing stupid," Chase said as he sat down. "Karma's a bitch, though. You know Millie's going to bring home some guy just like that."

"Man, shut the fuck up."

"My grandma always told me your kids give you back what you put out. If that's true, then Millie's going to date someone just like you. Lord help us all."

"First, we both know there's no one quite like me—"

"Thank God," Chase said, finishing the last of his whiskey.

"And second, if she did happen to find that rarest of all men," Mack said, grinning, "I would be happy to welcome him into the family with open arms."

"Be careful what you wish for," Chase said as he headed to the bar for a refill.

Chapter Five

"Mills? Where are you?" I hear Mason yelling from inside the house, and I already know I'm in trouble again. I'm usually done showering by the time he gets home from work. "Millie?"

He sounds like he's starting to panic. He's been overly protective of me since the day we met, but he's gone into full-on bodyguard hyper-drive since I was kidnapped. Despite doing everything in his power to be there to stop it from happening, he wasn't there and I almost died. Surprisingly, that's taken way more of a toll on him than it has on me.

"Millie!" I know he saw my car in the driveway, so there's no use trying to hide from him.

"I'm in the back, babe!" I yell over the sound of the water streaming over me from the outdoor shower on my back patio. I'm rinsing my hair when he walks through the French doors. He turns toward me and throws his hands up in exasperation.

"Millie! What did I tell you about showering naked outside?"

"That it's perfectly fine and I should definitely use my own judgment on the matter," I say, tilting my head and doing my best to smile sweetly.

"That's not even a little bit right," he says. He tries to keep his face stern, but his expression changes rapidly as his eyes start exploring my body. His voice lowers into a growl. "Can you please keep your swimsuit on until you get in the house?"

"I mean, I guess I could, but I don't really want to," I say, purposely challenging him again. My attempts to break him of his protective obsession have absolutely failed up to this point. From the look on his face, this one is failing, too. "Besides, no one can see me when I'm in the shower. These walls are like ten feet tall."

"They're eight feet tall, and if someone breaks into the backyard, it doesn't matter how high the walls are," he says as he starts to slowly walk into the shower.

"Apparently someone did just break in, and all he's doing so far is lecturing me."

He raises his eyebrows as he starts to smile. "Millicent. You're being very bad right now."

"Don't call me that." I made the mistake of telling him my grandma used to call me Millicent. He knows I don't like it. He uses it when he's scolding me.

I back up under the protection of the stream of water as he starts to close in. He's calculating each step like a cheetah stalking a gazelle on the Kenyan plains. He's still fully clothed from work, right down to his combat boots.

"Stop!" I say, laughing as I flick water at him from the shower stream. "Stop. You're going to get wet."

"Yeah. So are you." He lunges at me, coming directly through the water—spinning me around and pinning my frontside to the shower wall. He immediately puts his hand between my legs and strokes me with his fingers. "Hmm. Feels like you already are. Does just the sound of my voice make you this wet?"

"You know, when you're this arrogant, it's really a turn-off," I say, panting and trying desperately to sound convincing.

"Is that right?" He slowly snakes his hands around my body and starts playing with my already fully erect nipples. He starts gently kissing my neck, knowing just how to make me squirm. His hands move down my body and press my hips backward as he starts rhythmically grinding me into him. I nudge his kisses away from my neck and onto my lips. He pulls me closer to him as he starts exploring my mouth with his tongue.

He stops kissing me for a second and whispers, "You know your neighbors are going to hear us."

"Maybe," I say defiantly. "That depends entirely on if you can make me moan."

"Yeah, like that's ever been a problem," he says as he strokes me between my legs again. I let out a low moan.

"See?" he whispers.

"There's no way anyone heard that. You're going to have to try harder." I barely get it out before he pushes his fingers inside me. "Ahh!" My moan echoes off the shower walls.

"That's my girl," he says softly as he starts to kiss my neck again. His fingers start to pump in and out of me. He lets me enjoy the ride for a few minutes before he rubs his thumb directly on the spot he knows will make me finish the most quickly. My body shudders up against him after only a few expertly executed strokes.

With my body still tingling, he turns me around to face him. I pull off his drenched T-shirt and run my hands over his chest until I get to his belt. I quickly free him of his pants and start stroking him. He lifts me up and I push him inside me. I wrap my legs around his waist as he starts pumping himself into me. My body's so stimulated that it only takes a few strokes for me to cum again. He follows with a groan that slowly rumbles out from deep inside him.

He pulls me even closer—breathing heavily into my ear as the water continues to stream over his back. "I love you," he says, nuzzling my wet hair with his nose.

I bite his earlobe playfully. "I love you, babe."

He lifts me down gently and pushes me against the wall again. He places his arms on either side of me—his fingertips resting lightly on my head. He does this when he's trying to get me to conform to his way of thinking—like he's attempting a Vulcan mind meld.

"Millie. I don't want to have this argument again, but will you please stop showering outside when I'm not here? Please. Just rinse off the sand and go inside to take your full shower."

I put my hands on his cheeks and kiss him. "Mase, you've got to back off a little. We've talked about this. Between you and Chase, you're smothering me. I love you. But I took care of myself pretty well for twenty-five years."

He releases me and backs away as he pulls his pants up. "Eight years. You took care of yourself for eight years. Your dad took care of you before that, and Chase would have taken care of you those eight years if you wouldn't have been playing hide-and-seek with him." He nods his head as he grabs my towel off the hook and throws it to me. "Yeah. He told me how you unsuccessfully tried to shake him for all those years. I will go to my grave not understanding why you put up such a resistance to people trying to take care of you."

A chill runs through me as I hastily wrap myself in the towel. "Okay, first, I'm not really liking the bromance you and Chase have started. Stop talking to him about me. It makes me uncomfortable. And second—again—I don't need you or Chase to take care of me. I appreciate it. But I don't need it. You've got to start trusting me to take care of myself. Then what you offer can be an added bonus."

"God, I don't want to argue about this again," he says, rubbing his hands roughly over his face. "You know who I am. You know what I do for a living. I protect people. It's my job. I'm trying really hard to crank it down when I'm with you, but it's never going to go away completely. You can't get frustrated with me for being who I am."

I take a deep, cleansing breath and start toward the door. "I need to get dressed."

"Baby." He catches me by the arm and turns me back around to him.

"Mase, I don't want to argue about this, either. Can we just drop it? I'm not mad. I know you're working on it. And I know it's not easy. I appreciate the effort. Really, I do."

I smile weakly at him. He lets go of my arm. "Okay." He sighs as he turns toward the kitchen. "We're supposed be at the bar in an hour. Do you still want to go?"

"Yeah. It's fine."

I shut the bedroom door and slide down it until I'm curled up in a ball at the bottom. These past two months with Mason have been the most exhilarating days of my life. The way I love him makes me feel crazy. He fills me so full of emotion that most of the time I feel like an overly full balloon about to burst.

That's a good thing, right?

Chapter Six

When we get out of the car, Millie takes my hand and leads me toward the bar. I lag behind so I can watch her long blonde hair as it sways back and forth—giving me little peeks of the tanned skin her backless sundress exposes.

She knows this is my favorite dress. It's the one I want to rip off her the second she puts it on. The sheer-blue material cascades off her butt and flows all the way down her long legs. When she walks, it looks like gently rippling ocean waves. I'm thinking about how I'd like to be swimming in those waves when a jarring voice brings me out of my haze.

"Mason! So nice to see you!" Mariel laughs loudly as Millie and I walk to their table. "Chase, isn't it so nice to see him again?"

Annie and Charlie are already there, lounging at the other end of the table. They're laughing, too. Everyone's laughing except Chase, who has his head buried in his hands.

"Uh, what's happening here?" Millie wags her finger suspiciously at them.

I share her suspicions. Since I moved to San Diego, Chase and his friends have slowly accepted me as Millie's boyfriend, but they've never been this excited to see me.

"It's just that Chase saw you an hour or so ago, and here you are again," Mariel says, shoving Chase on the shoulder. Chase straightens up in his chair and shakes his head violently like he's trying to get rid of everything inside of it.

"Wait. You saw Mason an hour ago?" Millie says. She hasn't caught up with the conversation yet. Unfortunately, I think I have. Millie's been trying to break Chase of his habit of showing up to her house unannounced. I'm guessing by the anguish on his face he finally learned his lesson about an hour ago.

"Chase, are you going to tell her?" Mariel's staring at him with her perfectly honed I-told-you-this-was-going-to-happen face. Chase shakes his head again.

I pull Millie back against me and wrap my arms around her—partially to try to shield her from what she's about to hear, but mainly because I don't want her to hurt Chase.

"Babe," I say quietly, "I think Chase might have walked into your backyard again. Unannounced. Where the shower is. An hour ago . . ."

I don't even have to look at Millie's face to know it's tensed up as violently as her body has. "Oh my God! Chase! Did you see me showering?" She presses her body against me. I wrap my arms a little tighter around her. "Please tell me that didn't happen! Chase!"

Chase puts his face back in his hands—massaging his

temples—as he lets out a groan that sounds like something you'd hear from an animal caught in a trap.

Mariel stops laughing just long enough to say, "Well he didn't exactly see you showering . . ."

Charlie walks over and hands me what looks like a double shot of whiskey. I shoot it quickly.

Chase finally looks up. Through tightly clenched teeth, he says, "I came into the yard and heard a scream and . . . oh fuck. I can't do this. I'm going to go gouge my eyes out."

As Chase chugs the beer in front of him, Mariel says, "Mason, Chase saw your backside as you had Millie pressed up against the shower wall."

"Oh my God," Millie says, groaning. "Were we having sex? Chase! Seriously. I've told you to stop letting yourself into my yard."

She breaks free of me and shoves Chase on the shoulder on her way over to the chair on the other side of Mariel. She's glaring at him when he finally looks up at her.

"I will never go to your house again—even if I'm invited. I will never unsee what I saw today. The image of Mason's butt is permanently burned into my retinas," Chase says, rubbing his eyes vigorously.

Millie leans back in her chair, crossing her arms and shaking her head as she continues to glare at Chase. Mariel hands her a martini. She slams it and starts aggressively pulling the olives off the pick with her teeth.

"You know, to be real honest, I'd like to see Mason's butt," Annie says, laughing.

"Girl, cosign!" Mariel says as they exchange an air high-five across the table.

"C'mon, Mason. It will make Chase feel less awkward if you show all of us your butt," Annie says.

"Annie, I'm sitting right here," Charlie says, shaking his head.

"I know, baby," Annie says, patting her husband's arm.

"Seriously, I don't know what the big deal is," Charlie says. "It's not like you two aren't all over each other all the time. Really, we've all seen way too much."

"We're not all over each other all the time," Millie says as she whips her head around to Charlie.

"All. The. Time. Everywhere." Charlie leans back a little in his chair to clear himself out of Millie's slapping range. "I mean even when you're not touching, you're eye-fucking each other."

"All right. End of discussion," Millie orders. "Find something else to talk about."

She stands up and starts walking past me toward the bar.

"I'll get you another one," I say as I grab her empty martini glass.

She takes it back. "Thanks, but I can get it."

I pull her back gently and put my arms around her waist. I rest my head on her shoulder as we both look at the bar.

"Mills, look at the situation," I say, pointing at the group of disorderly men that are currently covering every inch of the bar. "Who's going to have a better chance of getting you a drink without getting touched? You or me?"

"Definitely me," she says without hesitation. She pulls at my arms to try to release them from around her.

I shake my head and sigh deeply as I release her. "Okay, Miss Independent. Go get 'em."

She walks confidently to the bar and starts working her way through the drunks. Some douche in a suit immediately grabs her by the shoulder and starts flirting with her.

I watch them for a few minutes until Charlie shoves me. "You notice the suit over there hitting on Millie?"

"Yep."

"And this restraint you're showing—is this part of the new give-Millie-more-space initiative?"

"Yes it is," I say, whistling a long breath out through my teeth.

"And on a scale of one to ten, how badly do you want to punch that guy right now?" He laughs as he looks down at my clenched fists.

"Ah, man, I passed ten the second he looked at her. I'm at about five thousand right now. Give or take a hundred."

"Well your restraint is impressive, brother," Charlie says, patting me on the back. "You think Millie's back-off order applies to me, too? Because I'm more than willing to go string that guy up by his tie."

"Sorry, man. I think it applies to anyone who wears a trident on his uniform."

"That's too bad." He pulls up a chair next to me to watch the show unfold.

Millie now has a scrum of drunks talking to her, and despite her best efforts, she hasn't made it any closer to the bar. She tries to squeeze through two of them, but gets rejected again as they close ranks. She turns slowly to look at me, and walks a few steps back toward us.

"Umm," she says, biting her lip. "I think I might need your help—just a little bit."

I don't even try to stop the smile that explodes on my face. "No, babe. You've got this. You were only a few feet from the bar."

"If you're trying to prove a point with this," she says, waving her hand in front of my face, "it's not working."

"What point could I possibly be trying to prove?" I lean back in my chair and fold my arms, still smiling broadly. "Go on. Go get your drink. You can do it."

"This is not a good look on you," she says, pressing her lips together in her best attempt not to smile.

She rolls her eyes at me and whips back around toward the bar—a new determination in her step. She makes it through the first layer of drunks. Since she's now in the middle of them, I don't see exactly what happens next, but the crowd parts in time for me to see Millie kneeing a guy in the balls.

When he crumples over, she puts her elbow hard into the back of his shoulder. She backs up into a defensive mode—her dress swaying wildly from side to side. Probably not the best outfit for a bar brawl. Before the guy recovers, I grab her around the waist and carry her back to our group.

"Okay, killer," I say. "That's plenty."

Her victim manages to stand upright again. "What the fuck?" he says as he points at Millie. "You need to learn how to take a joke."

Still holding Millie in one arm, I push him back with the other and then turn calmly toward Chase. I hand Millie to him. "You want to take care of this for me?"

"Yeah, I got her," he says, grabbing her arm as I put her down. He pulls her behind him and Charlie.

"I totally had him," Millie says to Chase, rubbing her elbow.

"I know, sweetie. You were really impressive." He puts his arm around her. "Let me see your elbow. Did you hurt it?"

Charlie puts his hands on her shoulders and looks at her intensely, like he's instructing a boxer on what to do in the next round. "Millie. When your victim leans over to grab his balls, instead of striking his shoulder, try putting a hard elbow right into his ear. It's a softer target for you, and it hurts your attacker like hell. Plus if you're lucky, the guy might lose his hearing."

Millie nods and gives him a fist bump. "Good tip, Charlie. My dad never taught me that."

Charlie nods thoughtfully. "Yeah. He was probably a more principled fighter than I am."

Chase laughs and shakes his head. "You obviously never met Mack."

From the corner of my eye, I see Millie's attacker trying to walk around me to get to her. I grab him and quickly wrap his arm behind him. I turn him to face his friends as I spread my fingers across his throat.

"All right," I say loudly to the group. "We've got two choices here. First choice: I'm one small move away from breaking his arm with my right hand. That's the most efficient choice—very quick, very easy. Or second choice: I'm two moves away from breaking his neck with my left hand. This choice is a little more complicated for me, but I'm more than willing to put in the extra effort if that's what you choose."

The drunks are suddenly quiet. A few of them look back at Chase and Charlie—probably trying to guess if they're going to join in if the group tries to overpower me. They look away pretty quickly, so I'm guessing they think the answer is yes.

"Or I'll add in a third choice just for you," I say as I pull up slightly on the guy's arm, causing him to wince. "I'll let him go—unharmed—if all of you leave the bar right now. Pay what you owe, leave generous tips for the bartender, and be on your way. This option expires in twenty seconds."

The group looks at me in stunned silence. Charlie walks up to stand next to me. "Did you say twenty seconds or twenty minutes? Because I'm not really getting a sense of urgency here."

"I said seconds, Charlie. And we're down to ten now." I pull up on the guy's arm again for emphasis.

Suddenly, there's a flurry of credit cards and cash flying at the bartender. I let the guy go and push him over to his friends.

"I need a dirty martini and a double whiskey when you have a second," I say to the bartender. "And let me know if they don't leave you at least twenty percent."

Millie's looking at me when I turn around.

"I know. I know. I'm in trouble again for protecting you," I say as I sit down and pull her onto my lap.

She puts her arm around my neck and whispers into my ear. "You're not in trouble right now, but I'm definitely going to have to discipline you when we get home tonight."

"Promise?" I say as I spread my hand over her butt and give it an ample squeeze.

As I start to kiss her, Charlie leans down inches from our faces and says loudly, "All. The. Time. Everywhere."

Chapter Seven

"Damn, Mack. You're shooting like a sniper today—all fifteen rounds right in the head," Chase said as he watched Mack empty his rifle into the target down range. "Must have been that visit from Carol last night."

Mack snapped his head toward Chase. "How'd you know she was here? You stalking me?"

"Believe me, I have no desire to know what you do on your free time. My wife, on the other hand . . ."

"So what? Mariel's stalking me?"

"I guess Mar and Carol are friends now."

"What? How'd that happen?"

"Apparently, that's what women do when you introduce them," Chase said, shaking his head. "I told you not to bring her around the bar unless you wanted everyone up in your business."

"They only talked for like two minutes that night. How does that work itself into friendship?"

"Mariel works fast. You already know that. And she wants you married off. Carol's the only decent woman you've brought around in, well, ever."

"We're not getting married. We're just friends."

"With benefits, apparently . . ."

"Wait. Carol told Mar we're having sex?"

"No, but you just told me," Chase said, laughing.

"You're an asshole."

"Like I don't know that already."

"Man, don't tell Millie about Carol," Mack said.

"How am I going to tell her anything? I literally have not seen that child since you brought her back from Bosnia. I still don't know why you don't bring her around here."

"I told you I don't want her anywhere near this base—near this life. This shit is totally separate from her. She's sweet and gentle. She doesn't need to know this life any more than she already does. Besides, I'm out in two months. Too late to bring her around now."

"Why don't you want her to know about Carol? Doesn't Millie like her?"

"She loves her. Carol's like the closest thing Millie has to a mother. She's been friends with Carol's daughter, Chloe, since she was about three."

"So why wouldn't she want you dating her?"

"She would want me dating her. In fact, she's told me to date her," Mack said as he ejected the empty mag and started taking his rifle apart to clean it. "I don't want to get her hopes up. Carol and I aren't getting married."

"Well, I can see if she doesn't want to marry you. She could do better."

"It's not like that. Millie and I are moving soon. Carol's entire family is in the Outer Banks or just around there. It wouldn't work out."

"And you'd have to give up your harem."

"I'd gladly give them up. That's just stress relief. Not even in the same class with Carol."

"I don't know, man. I saw the way she was looking at you at the bar. I think she'd move to California to be with you."

Mack shrugged. "Maybe. It's not time for that, though. We'll see what happens. Millie and I need to get out there first and get established. She's the most important thing, and then we'll see what happens."

"I get that. I'm looking forward to re-meeting Millie. You're going to let us around her out in San Diego, right?"

"You—definitely. I'm not so sure about Mar, though," Mack said, shaking his head. "I think Millie might be a little young for that kind of energy."

"You're way too protective of her. She's going to get to college and go hog wild. Got to let them experiment a little bit."

"Fuck you. You didn't let your daughters do shit when they were teenagers. And I'm not convinced you don't have them under surveillance at college."

Chase sighed. "I wish. Every time they come home for a visit, they're wearing less clothes. Mariel told me they wear more clothes than she did when I was chasing her."

"Is that supposed to make you feel better? I saw how you went after her."

"Right? Like I want some asshole pursuing my daughter like I did with Mar. I've always said we should start a business where retired SEALs keep an eye on active SEALs' daughters."

"Worst plan ever. Like we could trust them not to hit on our daughters themselves."

"Yeah. You're not wrong. I'm glad you and Millie are going to be out there with us, though. I'm struggling a little with hanging this all up. I'm not sure what I'm going to do with my time. It makes me nervous. Mar and I are already fighting about it."

"You'll figure it out. Mar's feisty, but she's crazy about you. She'll help you through it. And what she doesn't help you with, I'll pick up."

"You're going to help me? Like what? You going to go into therapy or something?"

"I'll help you drown your problems in beer and whiskey. Just like I do now."

"Appreciate it, brother," Chase said, chucking Mack on the shoulder. "Seriously, man. I don't know what I'd do without you."

Chapter Eight

"Do you want to get married?"

We're sitting on the back porch eating burritos. I'm thinking about how I wished I ordered extra guacamole.

Wait. What did Mason just say?

"What?" I mumble with my mouth still full of beans and cheese.

"Married, Millie. Do you want to get married?" He says it like it's the most normal question to ask right at this very moment.

"Are you proposing to me, or is this just a general conversation?" I say slowly, trying to give my brain enough time to catch up.

"Which do you want it to be?"

I finally look across the table at him to see if he's kidding. I'm desperately hoping to see the twinkle that lights up his crystal-blue eyes when he's teasing me. It's not there.

"I'm not sure that's the way it works." I try to keep my

tone casual so it doesn't reflect the panic that's starting to surge through my body. "It's either a proposal or it's not."

I've only seen his eyes look this intense once, and that was seconds before an enemy force started firing on us. It happened six months ago and only a few weeks after we met. So much has happened since then. Most days it seems like a lifetime ago, but now, with those battle-ready eyes staring at me, it feels like yesterday.

His eyes suddenly soften. From the day I met him, Mason's been able to read my mind. Right now, he's definitely sensing my panic. "Let me back it up a little," he says in the soothing tone he uses when he thinks I'm about to overreact to something. It works on me like the sound of the ocean works on most people.

"So not a proposal?" I sigh, relieved at the bullet I just dodged.

"I didn't say that," he says gently.

"Mase, we haven't even known each other a full year. Don't you think it's too early to think about marriage?"

He reaches across the table and takes my hand. "In the past half year: we met, survived a brutal firefight, took out a terrorist network, moved to the same city, and fell in love. How is anything we've done so far on a normal timeline?"

"That's just it," I say, pushing my half-eaten burrito away from me. "Nothing we've done is normal, so why do we have to get married and be normal? What we have is just as good— if not better—than marriage."

"So you don't want to marry me?" He tries to hide his disappointment with a half-hearted laugh.

"Babe, I told you the other day. This has nothing to do

with you. I need some time to figure out me—what I want to do—before I can figure out anything else."

"Yeah. I know. I heard what you said. I thought getting married would give you more solid footing in one area of your life."

I walk around the table, sit on his lap, and rest my head on his shoulder. He wraps his arms around me and kisses the top of my head.

"We've never talked about marriage before," I say softly. "I didn't even know it was something you wanted."

"Yeah, I want it. I want it with you for sure. You don't want it?"

"I don't know. I guess marriage has never been important to me. I haven't really thought about it much."

"It seems like a deeper commitment to me. You know? Like we're locking it in." His face starts nuzzling my hair. "And if we have kids, I think it's better for them."

I sit up quickly, almost falling off his lap. "Wait. So now we're having kids?"

"I mean, yeah, I want kids. I'm thirty-five. I'd like to have a few kids before I'm too old."

I shake my head, hoping to clear the swirling tornado that's rapidly forming. The shaking makes the tornado stronger. I try to stand up, but fall back against Mason's legs.

"Baby, settle down," he says, steadying me. "We're just having a conversation. Yeah. I want to get married and have kids, but I'm not saying it has to happen today. I know you didn't grow up around happy marriages. Your dad was never married. Your grandma was never married. But people do have good marriages—a lot of people. Look at Chase and Mariel."

"Mase, your first marriage ended in divorce." I unsuccess-fully try to stop the words from coming out of my mouth.

He stands up, pushing me up with him as he starts walking away. "Oh, so that's what you're worried about. You're not worried about marriage in general. You're worried about whether I can make a marriage work."

"That's not what I meant, Mason," I say, following him toward the house.

He turns around. "What did you mean? Tell me exactly what you meant."

"I meant what I said. I love you. But I'm not ready for marriage. And I'm definitely not ready for kids. And it doesn't have anything to do with how I feel about you. I'm sorry if you feel differently. Maybe I'll change my mind, but I'm defi-nitely not ready for that right now."

"Fine. Let's stop talking about it."

I follow him into the house. "Mase. We can't keep ignoring things we disagree on. We need to talk about this stuff. You completely shut down when you don't get your way."

"When I don't get my way?" He whips around to face me. "I'm not a toddler throwing a tantrum because I can't stay up a little later. I asked you to marry me and you said no."

"Well, you didn't actually ask me," I say, laughing and trying desperately to lighten the mood.

"Oh, okay." He walks over to me swiftly, grabbing my hand and dropping down on one knee. "Will you marry me? There, I've officially asked you."

"Mason. Stop. Why are you being like this?"

"I officially asked you. Now you have to officially

answer." He stands up and drops my hand. "Say no if you don't want to marry me."

"No, I don't want to get married. And it has nothing to do with you. I just don't want to get married."

He shakes his head as he turns around. "I need to run some errands. And I think I'm going to stay at my place tonight."

"Mason." I make a feeble attempt to stop him from charging out of my house. The door closes loudly behind him. I turn around to look at the porch table—now cluttered with half-eaten burritos. I collapse against the wall, wondering how I got from wanting more guacamole to possibly ruining my entire future in less than five minutes.

Chapter Nine

MASON, SAN DIEGO, CALIFORNIA, 2020

Chase opens his front door and reads my face and body language instantly—exactly the way we were taught to read the enemy. As a special forces operator, you can't take much time to guess someone's intentions—you must evaluate quickly and act immediately. Chase's eyes tell me if he had a gun handy, he would have already shot me.

"I think I fucked up," I say, not breaking my stare with him.

Chase's eyes sink into attack mode. "I swear to God, Mason, if you cheated on her, I'm cutting off your dick right here and now."

"I didn't cheat on her," I say as I drop down on the bench on his porch. "I asked her to marry me."

"Oh yeah, well you really have gone too far now," Chase says, rolling his eyes as he walks out on the porch, letting the door slam behind him.

"No, man. You don't know. It really freaked her out. She

got all panicky. And I kept going at her. I couldn't quit. Like I had to prove a point. I think I fucked it up for real this time."

"You didn't fuck anything up," he says, sighing deeply. "She's fully in love with you. It's just, you know, Millie's not like other girls. She didn't spend her childhood imagining her perfect wedding. Mack had her playing with guns and night-vision goggles—not wedding dresses and flowers. Maybe marriage isn't her thing. It doesn't mean she doesn't want to be with you."

"I know. Everything comes back to her dad. I think she's turning a corner and learning to live without him, and then something else comes up—like he wasn't married, so she doesn't want to be."

"Uh, I think you're reading that wrong. I don't think it has much to do with Mack not being married. It's more the bond she had with him. I think it's impossible for anyone to get to Millie's inner circle of trust. Believe me, I've been trying for years. That place is reserved for Mack only. And when he left her so suddenly, it closed all-together. I don't think you're ever going to get there. And if I know anything for sure about Millie, the more pressure you put on her, the more she absolutely shuts down."

I lean back and close my eyes. "It's like I start to make progress, and then I run smack into another wall. It's so frustrating. I was close to my mom, but not like this. I can't figure it out."

"From the little you've told me, I know losing your mom was hard, but you still had your dad and brother. In fact, you still have them to this day. When Mack died, Millie didn't have anyone. Her grandma died soon after that, and Camille was worthless anyway. Mar and I tried to be there for her, but as I told you, she practically eliminated us from her life. These last few months are the closest I've ever felt to Millie. I think you've been good for her. Whether you recognize it or not, she's changing for the better."

"You think?"

"I know. The fact she's trusting us enough to have her back—even a little bit—is such a huge step forward for her. You're doing that. She trusts you."

"Yeah, I guess. She's complicated, man. Not like any woman I've ever known before. She makes me crazy."

"All the good ones do, brother." He stands up and heads to the door. "You want a beer?"

"No. I need to go back over to Millie's and apologize. I was an asshole. I need to at least try to make it right," I say as I stand up slowly. "You know she told me she hates when we talk about her."

"Yeah, well Millie doesn't get to control everything. You're welcome over here any time with or without her."

When I get back to Millie's house, I don't know if I should use my key or knock. I decide to use the key. All the lights are off in the house, but her car's in the driveway. I peek in the bedroom and see her sleeping under the mass of blankets.

I stand there and watch her for a little bit. It makes me think back to the first time we shared a bed after we survived the firefight. I stayed with her all night to make sure her concussion didn't get worse. I was into her from the first second I saw her, but that was the night I fell in love with her —watching her sleep so innocently, all curled up in a little ball like she is now.

I crawl under the blankets. She opens her eyes, looking a little bit confused.

"I'm sorry, Mills. I overreacted. I was an asshole." I reach out to touch her shoulder. "Is it okay if I stay? I wouldn't blame you if you didn't want me here."

She scoots toward me and turns around—spooning her body into me. Just like she did that first night. I wrap my arms around her tightly and kiss the top of her head.

"So you're rescinding the proposal," she says softly.

"Nothing's rescinded. It's just put way in the back of the shelves. Behind all the kitchen stuff we never use. Maybe one day we'll take it out; maybe we won't. But married or not, I know—with certainty—I never want to let you go." I squeeze her tighter. "Is that okay?"

"Yeah," she says as she turns back around to face me. "Can I ask you something?"

"Are you going to ask me to marry you?"

"Stop," she says, kissing my nose. "No. It's just . . . are you happy?"

"Baby, I'm so happy. You know that. Why are you asking?"

"I know how much you miss leading your team. If you want to go back for a few months to fill in, I'll come with you."

"I'm not going to lie to you. I miss it badly. But that life is no way to live if you want to have a successful relationship—especially if you're just starting one like we are. You'd rarely see me. You would be alone most of the time. It would be bad for you and for me."

She rolls over on her back and looks at the ceiling. "You're right. I know. But this bubble we've been living in is going to pop at some point. I need to get a job. You need to enjoy your job. The real world's going to set in."

I put my hand on her stomach and start rubbing the knot I know is forming. "That entire speech is out of Mariel's mouth. Right?"

She laughs. "Yeah."

"I've told you before what works for them isn't necessarily what's best for everyone. We can stay in this goddamn bubble forever if it works for us."

She turns her head to me and smiles—a little sparkle in her eyes.

"And you don't have to decide what you want to do with the rest of your life right now," I say, stroking her cheek. "You've gone through so much. Be patient with yourself."

She lets out a long sigh and nuzzles her face into my chest. "It's been six months. I've basically been surfing and sleeping all that time. I have to figure out what I'm going to do at some point. I feel like there's something coming. The idea keeps dashing through my head, but I can't understand it yet."

"Take a breath. Really, you don't have to do anything. With the money you made on your grandma's house sale, you're financially set. And I have money. If you want to just surf, God knows you've earned it. With everything that's happened, you've lived like four lives in only twenty-five years."

"Before all this happened—before Dad died—I wanted to major in marine conservation and save the ocean from all the evil polluters in the world," she says, shaking her head against my chest. "I was more idealistic back then."

"Mills, you can still do that. You're so young. And we live in San Diego—the perfect place for it. I've spent a lot of time in oceans. I've seen all the crap that ends up there. We need more people like you to do something about it. You'd be great. But you don't have to worry about that or marriage or babies or any of it. Let's just enjoy the bubble for as long as we want to."

"Can we take naps in the bubble?"

"As many as we want. Any time we want," I say as I turn her back around into a spoon. "In fact, let's start on that right now."

Chapter Ten

MILLIE! Are you going to text me that you made it home ok or am I going to have to send out a search party?!!!

Mack stared at his text. He sent it after calling her twice. Both calls went straight to voicemail. It had been almost two hours since Millie left the base after she showed up unexpectedly in the afternoon.

At the most, it should take an hour for her to get back home. Mack told her to text when she got there. She hadn't yet. He started worrying when the clock hit exactly one hour, and now he was in full-blown panic mode.

After she left, his team had been briefed on a few missions in Iraq. They were wheels up in a few days. He sat in his car wondering how he could follow her route home, check every ditch he was sure she was lying in, and still get back in time to leave for Iraq. His phone finally beeped.

DAD!! Omg. I'm sorry!! I stopped at Kaylee's house on the way home. I forgot.
My bad! Call off the search party. I'm back home. Love you. xxoo

Mack took a deep breath and laughed. She would be the death of him. He was sure about that. He wondered daily how his child could be so unaffected by things like time. His entire life was based on order, and he was raising a daughter who had absolutely no sense of it. As much as it almost drove him to the edge, it was still his favorite thing about her. She was care-free—the exact opposite of him—and he loved every last bit of it.

Glad you're back safely, sweetie. Love you. See you this weekend. xxoo

Mack's mind was still full of Millie when he unlocked his apartment door. Normally, he would have noticed the new scratches around the lock. He was trained to notice small details like that. He didn't notice them though, so he was taken by surprise when he heard a voice coming from his living room.

"Millie's life is in danger." It was a man's voice with a very heavy Slavic accent.

Muscle memory took over as Mack fluidly took his pistol out of his waist-band and dropped to a knee behind the protection of the entryway table. There was a little light coming through the blinds, so he could just see the outline of a man sitting on the couch—his arms crossed on his lap with no detectable weapon. Mack had an easy shot at his head. He decided not to take it.

Mack kept the pistol pointed at the man. "Stand up," Mack ordered.

The man stood up and raised his arms above his head.

When Mack flipped the lights on, he could see the man was about his age. Maybe a little older. He was wearing a crisply pressed shirt and trousers. "Pull up your shirt and turn around slowly," Mack said as he stood up.

"I don't have on an explosive belt," the man said as he lifted his shirt and carefully turned around.

"Up against the wall—hands overhead, feet spread."

The man did as he was told. Mack searched him for weapons as he kept his gun pressed to the man's head. When Mack was sure he was clean, he grabbed the man by the back of the collar and forced him to sit at the kitchen table. Mack remained standing—his gun at the ready.

"Put your hands on the table where I can see them," Mack said gruffly. "Who are you?"

"My name is Amar Petrovic. I'm the person who called to tell you about Millie sixteen years ago."

Mack's mind flashed back to receiving that call. A man called to tell him a baby had resulted from an affair Mack had in Bosnia. Mack went to Bosnia, basically kidnapped Millie, and brought her back to the United States. He waited nervously for years for someone to show up and try to take her back. No one ever had. He thought she was safe after sixteen years. Apparently, he was wrong.

"Why are you here now? And what do you mean Millie's in danger?" Mack said, glaring at Amar.

"When Nejra became pregnant, she told everyone—including me—she had been raped and that she didn't know the identity of her attacker. Everyone except one person—her aunt Azayiz. When Nejra was murdered, Azayiz feared the baby would be killed, too. She gave me your name and number with the instructions to call you and tell you to rescue the baby."

"I did that. Millie's safe. No one has ever tried to locate her." Mack put his gun back in his waistband.

"Until now, no one cared. Her uncle Sayid was actually grateful you took her. You know who he is now—a terrorist. But when Millie was born, he was not yet cold-blooded. The elders were pressuring him to kill the baby. He never could have done that to his sister. Nejra was his world."

"So what changed his mind? I'm assuming you think he's coming after her now."

"No, not Sayid. Yusef Hadzic. The three of us were child-hood friends. Yusef followed Sayid into the terrorist network. I fled Bosnia for Spain. I've done my best over the past fifteen years to eliminate them completely from my life. But last week, Azayiz contacted me. She moved back to her native Pakistan after her husband was killed in the Bosnian War." Amar paused and took a deep breath. "Since returning, she has been an informant for the CIA. I didn't know that until last week. She has apparently been informing on Sayid's network for years. Her son, Fareed, is part of the network. I think he's been providing her information. Yusef found out about it and has put a bounty on her head. The CIA moved her into protective custody. She told me last week Yusef was trying to draw her out of hiding by targeting the one person in this world she would die protecting—your daughter."

Mack sat down at the table. He stared at Amar for a few minutes before responding. "Why would a woman who hasn't seen Millie in sixteen years care whether she lives or dies?"

"When Nejra's parents died at the beginning of the war, Azayiz became like a mother to her. When Nejra was murdered, all the love Azayiz felt for her was transferred to Millie."

Mack took a second to process the information. "So what are you telling me? Yusef is coming for Millie? She's pretty safe here in the States."

"I've been following Millie for the last two days. She isn't as safe as you think."

Mack shoved the table hard against Amar's ribs. He leapt up and grabbed Amar's crumpled body and slammed him against the wall. "What did you say?" Mack said into Amar's face. "You've been following my daughter?"

"I would never hurt her," Amar said quickly. "Nejra was my best friend."

Mack threw Amar back down in the chair and shoved his

finger in his face. "Stay the fuck away from Millie. Do you hear me? I will kill you."

"I'm not your problem." Amar tried to bring his tone back down to a controlled level. "I wanted to see if someone could find her, and I found out they can. As I said, only Azayiz and I know your name. Yusef does not. I'm here to warn you he has started digging. I can't imagine he will figure out easily who you are. Yusef is not that bright. But if he finds out who you are, he is only one step away from Millie. I don't care about you, but I will always love Nejra. And I will do anything I can to protect her daughter. I would think her father would be prepared to do the same thing."

Mack sat back down. "Where are they? Sayid and Yusef? No one has been able to locate them in almost two decades. Tell me where they are, and we'll take them out."

"I don't know where they are. I don't want to know," Amar said quietly. "I don't want them to know where I am. If I did know, I would tell you. I have no allegiance to them anymore."

"So what are you asking me to do? Go into hiding? I'm guessing you know what I do for a living. I can't very well do that."

"I'm not asking you to do anything. I'm delivering a message from Azayiz. You're in danger. Millie is in danger. It's just a matter of time before they find you and then her. I don't want her to die, but it's out of my hands now. I've done what I promised to do." Amar put his hands on the table and slowly stood up. "I would like to leave now if you will allow it."

Mack nodded toward the door. Amar instinctively put his hands in the air as he walked past Mack.

As he opened the door, Amar said, "She looks like Nejra."

"I know." Mack paused as he tried to clear the lump that was quickly forming in his throat. "Thank you for calling to tell me about Millie. She's the only reason I have any happiness."

Amar turned around and smiled slightly at Mack before he closed the door behind him.

Chapter Eleven

MILLIE, SAN DIEGO, CALIFORNIA, 2020

"Dad? Where are you?"

We landed in San Diego a few hours ago, and we've already looked at three houses. We're on our fourth house now —a cute little bungalow near Pacific Beach. We're moving here soon and Dad told me I get to choose the house. I'm standing in the street, looking at the front. Dad disappeared inside somewhere.

"Millie. I'm here, sweetie. I'm inside. Come and find me." *It's his voice, but it sounds really distant. He must be down in the basement. I try to walk to the house, but my feet aren't moving for some reason. I look down to make sure they're still attached.*

"Dad, I'll be there in a second!" I yell, hoping he can hear me above the loud rumbling sound that has just started. I try to move my feet again, with no luck.

"Millie? Where are you? I'm here!" I can barely hear him

now, even though I can tell he's screaming. The rumbling sound has turned into a roar.

"I'm coming to find you!" I scream at the top of my lungs. As I try to throw my body forward to get my feet moving, a violent gust of wind blows me backward into the street. I fall down and hit my head hard against the curb. As the darkness starts to surround me, I hear the house blow up. I suddenly see Dad's body flying toward me. "Millie! Help me! Help me!" he screams as he passes over me.

I reach up to try to catch him. "Dad! Dad! Daaaaaaadddd . . ."

"Millie. Wake up." I open my eyes to see Mason inches from my face. He's shaking me gently. "You're having another bad dream. It's okay, baby. Wake up."

I take a sharp breath in and look around the room quickly to see if my dad's here. He's not. I'm in my bedroom in San Diego. Mason's here. Dad isn't. I have to remind myself Dad is still dead.

Mason pulls me up and presses my shoulders back against the headboard. He's still shaking me gently. "Mills. Look right here at me. You're awake now. The dream is over."

As my eyes start filling with tears, I nod my head so he knows I heard him. He pulls me to his chest and wraps his arms around me tightly. "It's okay, baby. You're okay. It's over. No one's going to hurt you." He kisses the top of my head as he rocks me back and forth slowly.

My head's spinning as I try to remember what's happening. I used to have these nightmares almost every night. I've only had a few in the two months Mason has been practically living with me. I was beginning to think they were leaving me for good. The thought of them returning makes me shudder. Mason squeezes me tighter.

"Do you want to talk about it? You were yelling for your dad. You haven't done that before," Mason whispers gently in my ear. "Was the dream different from the other ones?"

I pull back from his hug and lean against the headboard again. He wipes away my tears and reaches down to hold my hands.

"I haven't had this one before. Dad's never talked to me in the dreams. It's always just him blowing up in a house. You know? The way he died. And it always looks like it's in Iraq where it actually happened. This dream was *this* house blowing up, and he was yelling at me to find him. I tried to get to him, but I couldn't move. What do you think that means?"

He brushes the hair out of my face and strokes my cheek gently. "I don't think it means anything. It's just a dream. Your subconscious is mixing past and present. You know how weird dreams can be sometimes. Most of my dreams don't make any sense at all."

"Yeah, I know," I say, curling my legs up against me. "It felt like he was trying to tell me something. Do you think it's possible for dead people to talk to you in dreams?"

"I don't know, Mills. It's never happened to me. I used to dream about my mom all the time. She talked in the dreams, but I never really felt like she was trying to send me a message. It was like I was reliving a memory or something. But you know, she didn't die violently like your dad did, so maybe your dreams about him are more powerful than mine were."

"Yeah, I feel like it was an omen or something. It's creepy." Just as I finish saying it, a loud banging noise makes me dive under the covers.

"Mills," Mason says, pulling the covers back from my head. "Babe. Breathe. It's just someone knocking on the front door."

"What time is it?" I say, looking for my phone.

"Just before six. Are you expecting anyone?" He pulls the nightstand drawer open, where he keeps his loaded pistol.

"No, not at six in the morning." I reach for his hand to pull it away from the gun. "I'm sure you don't need that. Right?"

He gives me a stern look, but closes the drawer without getting the gun. "Stay here. I'll see who it is."

As I get out of bed to put on my robe, I hear a familiar voice coming from the living room.

"I'm looking for Millie Marsh. Does she live here?"

"Who's asking?" Mason grumbles.

"What are you, her bodyguard? Does she live here or not?"

Before Mason has a chance to reply, I fly around the corner. "George? Oh my God. What are you doing here?"

"You haven't returned any of my phone calls, so I thought I'd come find you," he says as he unsuccessfully tries to move around Mason.

"That's called stalking, George. It's against the law."

Mason pushes me behind him instinctively.

"No, Mase. Bad choice of words. He's not really stalking me. Like in the dangerous sense, anyway. This is my old boss from the agency, George Chapman. George, this is my boyfriend, Mason Davis."

Mason's still blocking the entrance, but somehow George squeezes his body into the house and hugs me. "Your boyfriend? Really? What happened to Dave back in D.C.?"

"His name was Drew, and we broke up a long time ago," I say, pulling out of the hug. "What are you doing here? What do you want?"

"Can I sit down?" George says, eyeing Mason cautiously. "Or is your new boyfriend going to try to kill me?"

"You can come in, but no guarantees on what Mason's going to do. He's a free spirit."

George sits on the couch and pats the cushion on the seat next to him. I purposely sit in the chair across from him.

"Haven't changed a bit, have you? Still as obstinate as ever." He pauses for a second, and looks up at Mason who's standing behind my chair. "Is there any way the bodyguard can leave? What I have to say is classified."

"He's a SEAL. He has clearance. He can stay."

George lets out a huge and unexpected wave of laughter as he takes off his glasses. "Wait. What?" he manages to get out. "You're dating a SEAL? A SEAL? After everything you went through with your dad. Seriously? I thought you disavowed everything about the teams."

Mason takes a large step toward him. I grab his leg. "Mase. He's harmless. Will you sit, please?" Mason takes the chair next to me, his eyes not leaving George. I'm suddenly very relieved I made him leave his gun in the bedroom.

"George, why are you here?" I say with frustration and fatigue dripping from my voice.

"I really can't talk about this, Millie. Not in front of him." George motions toward Mason. "It's for agency ears only."

"I don't work for the agency anymore."

"Since when? You're still getting paid."

"And I've asked you to have that stopped. The money's sitting in my bank account, ready to return to the agency. I've sent you two letters of resignation."

"I didn't accept your resignation and I still don't. As far as I'm concerned, you still work for us. For me."

"Well you can think anything you want, but I don't." I stand up to get some coffee. It's way too early in the morning for George.

George stands up and follows me. "Millie, this has to do with your family," he whispers. "Your overseas family . . ."

I turn around to see George right behind me and Mason right behind him. "Mason knows everything about my Bosnian family. You might as well start talking if you want to tell me something. He's not leaving." Mason purposely bumps George as he walks by him to hand me the hazelnut creamer out of the refrigerator.

"Fine." George sighs. "What do you know about Azayiz Custovic?"

"Nothing. I've never heard that name," I say, taking a long sip of coffee.

"She's your mother's aunt—your great-aunt."

"Okay. So is she dead? Why do I care about this?"

"She's not dead. She's originally from Pakistan. She had an arranged marriage with your great-uncle, and moved to Bosnia after the wedding." George starts tapping his fingers on the kitchen counter. Finger tapping is his tell. He does it when he's about to embellish something.

"I'm still not seeing what this has to do with me," I say cautiously. "You know I don't want anything to do with that side of my family."

George looks warily at Mason, still clearly not comfortable with him being a part of this conversation. "After you eliminated Sayid Custovic and Yusef Hadzic, there was a lull in the action from their network. We thought it was dead. But now, we're starting to see an uptick of activity from them again. We think Azayiz's son, Fareed, is running the show now. He grew up with Sayid and Yusef."

"Well first, I didn't eliminate anyone. Sayid had one of his people kill Yusef and then killed himself. And second, you're the one who taught me these networks never really die, they just get new leadership. So find Fareed. This has nothing to do with me."

"Unfortunately for both of us, it does have something to do with you." George's finger tapping is so loud now that it sounds like he's just been given a drum solo in his high school band. "Long story short, Azayiz has been working as an agency informant since 1995. In 2011, Yusef found out and put a bounty on her head. We've had her in hiding since then."

"Still not seeing where I come in." I walk to the back patio and take a seat directly in the sun. I close my eyes and try to wish George away.

"Mills," Mason says. I open my eyes to find him standing in the doorway behind George. "I need to jump in the shower. You okay with him?"

"Yeah, babe. He's just annoying, not dangerous."

"I'm standing right here, Millie," George says. "And do we have to sit outside? You know I don't like light."

I inhale deeply and close my eyes again. I hear him noisily pull one of the chairs to the shady side of the patio.

"As I was saying," he continues, "we've had her in hiding, but she disappeared last week."

I open my eyes. He has me mildly interested. "What do you mean disappeared? Did she leave on her own? Or was she kidnapped?"

"We definitely thought she was taken because we couldn't imagine why she would leave. She knows all too well how dangerous it is for her on the streets. But now we think she might have left on her own. We don't know why, but we need to find her. If she gets in the wrong hands, the best thing that can happen is that they kill her. She knows so much about our Middle East operations. If they interrogate her—and break her—it would be devastating to our work over there."

"So you want me to find her? I'm sure you have agents on the ground there who are in a much better position to do that."

"No, we don't want you to find her. We want her to find you." He looks at me like he's just given me the final clue to solve a puzzle.

"I don't know what that means. Does she even know who I am?"

"Oh she knows. Azayiz was very close to your mother, particularly after your grandparents died. She became almost like a big sister to her. When your mother was killed, she was devastated. It was Azayiz who alerted your dad of your exis-tence and arranged for him to take you out of Bosnia."

"Amar Petrovic called my dad. I confirmed that with him when I interrogated him in Sarajevo."

"Yes, Amar made the call, but Azayiz initiated it. She was the only one who knew who your dad was. She told Amar and asked him to call. She wanted to get you out of Bosnia—far from your uncle Sayid."

"Well I owe her for that, but I'm still not seeing what I can do to help you find her."

"Millie, she hasn't see you since you were a newborn. You're the only thing that remains of her precious niece. We think she would do anything to see you again."

"What am I supposed to do? Walk up and down a bunch of streets in Pakistan until she sees me?"

"Who's going to Pakistan?" I look over to see a freshly showered Mason standing in the doorway.

"Apparently I am," I say, rolling my eyes. "To act as bait to lure my great-aunt—who I've never met—out of hiding."

Mason walks over and hands me a fresh cup of coffee. "Yeah, that's not happening."

"Maybe we let Millie decide for herself," George says, scooting his chair back to get his legs out of the sun.

"Millie has decided for herself," I say as I grab Mason's arm to stop him from moving any closer to George. "And it's what Mason said—definitely not going to happen."

I look over to see George vigorously massaging his left temple with his ring finger. That's our old signal for 'Can't talk about it here. Meet me in the elevator.'

George stands up abruptly. "Well if you really don't want to work on this, I guess I can't force you. I can show myself out."

I definitely know he was giving me the signal now because he's never given up that easily on anything. George walks out the front door without saying another word. Mason closes the door behind him.

"That's who you reported to at the agency?" Mason says, laughing. "He doesn't seem like he's all there. I'm glad you got away from him."

Mason heads to the kitchen as I say as nonchalantly as possible, "Hey. I think I'm going to get changed and go for a run."

"You want me to come with you?"

"No, I'm good. I won't be very long. I need to clear my head after all that," I say, waving my hands at the door.

He makes his way back over to me. "You okay?"

"Yeah, I'm good. Really."

He hugs me and kisses the top of the head. "Okay, babe. Take your phone in case I need to find you."

"Mase, I'm not going to get kidnapped. That was so six months ago," I say, trying to make a joke. From the look on his face, I've failed miserably again.

"That's not funny, Millie. Take your phone. Please."

Chapter Twelve

George's car is nowhere to be seen when I leave the house, but I know he's lurking around somewhere. I start jogging down to the beach in case Mason's watching. When I turn the corner to take a shortcut through a parking lot, someone grabs me from behind and shoves me into a town car. I don't fight because I know who it is. I land in the back seat and see George smiling up at his driver, who I now recognize as Ted— George's henchman from the agency.

"Hey, Millie," Ted says, smiling. "Hope I didn't hurt you. George didn't want to take any chances of you ignoring him again."

"All good, Teddy," I say as he closes the door.

I turn to George. "What the fuck is wrong with you? Do you not remember I was shoved into a car at gunpoint less than a year ago? You're going to give me PTSD."

"Wait. Do you have PTSD? Really? Because if you do, I

can't tell you any of this. You know the old agency saying: 'Only sound minds can hear the crazy stuff.'"

"That's not an agency saying. It's a George saying. And I don't have PTSD yet. But years from now, I'm sure I'm going to fall to the ground shaking and crying any time I hear the name George."

"I think my ex-wife already does that. I can put you in touch with her if you want to know when to expect the onset."

"George," I say impatiently, "why did you give me the ring-finger signal? What more do you have to tell me?"

He looks away and sighs. He can't even make eye contact with me. That hasn't happened once in all the years I've known him. It must be something really good. Or something really bad. I'm not sure I want to hear it either way.

"Are you really dating that caveman back there? Seems like you could do better," he says, trying to change the subject.

"Not that it's any of your business, but he's not a caveman. He's kind and gentle and thoughtful. And he's amazing in bed."

"Ahh, Millie!" he says, covering his ears. "C'mon. I'm like your work dad. I don't need to hear that."

"You brought it up. And I already have a dad—well, had one. And he was perfect. I don't need you to fill in for him. Now what is it you want to tell me so badly that you had Teddy practically assault me?"

George sighs again—deeply this time—and then turns to face me with a wide-eyed expression I've never seen from him. "Well, speaking of your dad . . ."

I'm standing at Chase's front door. I have no idea how I got here or how long I've been staring at the doorbell. *Did I ring it yet?* I press it because it seems like the right thing to do, but I'm not sure what to say if he opens the door. *Why am I here?* My brain feels like it's frozen. I shake my head to try to clear the fog, but that makes me dizzy. When Chase opens the door, I'm struggling to stay standing.

"Hey!" he says. "I didn't know you were coming over today."

Yeah, neither did I. I was hoping he would be able to tell me why I'm standing at his front door, but it looks like we're both clueless. The smile on his face quickly disappears. He takes a step toward me. I still don't think I've said anything to him.

"Millie," he says as he grabs my shoulders. "Are you okay, sweetie? What's wrong?"

The dizziness is starting to take over. I close my eyes and fall backward.

"Millie!" Chase yells as he pulls me into a bear hug to steady me. As I let my body fall into his, I feel him lifting me up. The next thing I know, I'm lying on his couch shivering. He grabs the blanket hanging over the back of the couch and covers me with it.

"Millie." He's shaking my chin lightly. "You fainted. Can you focus on my eyes? That's good. Just relax. You're okay."

"Where am I?" I try to sit up. He pushes me gently back down.

"You're at my house. How did you get here? Your car isn't in the driveway. Did Mason drop you off? And you're soaking wet. How did you get so wet?"

I'm just starting to feel the pain radiating through my knees and ankles. "I think I might have jogged here."

"What do you mean 'you think'? And where did you jog here from?"

It's starting to come back to me a little. I remember leaving my house to go jogging. I remember Mason telling me to take my phone. "My house. I think," I say, looking at Chase and hoping he can confirm that for me.

"Millie, that's ten miles and mainly uphill. It's so hot this morning. No wonder you look like you're about to die. You probably have low blood sugar again. Did you eat before you started? I've told you to carbo-load before you jog or you're going to keep crashing."

He's made it over to the kitchen, where he's pouring me a glass of orange juice. He brings it to me with a jar of almonds. He pulls me up by my shoulders until I'm sitting half-way up, propped up on the pillows he's fluffing behind me. "You need to get some sugar back in your system. Here. Drink. And eat some almonds, too. I'm going to get you some dry clothes."

As the juice starts to enter my system, my brain snaps out of the fog and I remember the rest of it—meeting with George first at my house and then in his car. I remember what he told me when we were in his car, and it makes me start shaking again. I drop the jar of almonds and watch it hit my lap before it tumbles to the floor shattering on impact—sending almonds flying everywhere.

Chase is walking down the stairs with fresh clothes. He jumps down the last five stairs as the jar hits the ground. He's running toward me—hopping through the shattered glass and almonds like he's making his way through a minefield. He finally lands on the couch beside me.

He grabs my shoulders. "Millie!"

I look up at him—tears starting to rapidly form in my eyes. "Chase. Is Dad alive?"

"What? Millie. What's wrong with you?" He shakes my shoulders gently. "Are you hallucinating? I think I need to take you to the hospital."

"George told me he was alive." I start to shake again.

"What are you talking about? Who is George?"

"My boss from the agency. He was at my house this morning. I just left him. He told me Dad might still be alive—that he was alive after the day of the explosion."

Chase's mouth is wide open. He stares at me like he thinks I've completely lost it. "Millie," he says slowly, "are you being serious right now? No. Mack is not alive. You know that. And I don't know who this George guy is or why he's telling you that, but I do know, he wasn't there when Mack died. I was. I watched it happen. Your dad is not alive."

As my brain starts to focus again, I remember everything George said. "Did you find Dad's body that day?"

Chase lets go of my shoulders and looks down. "He's dead, Mills. He's dead."

"Answer my question."

Chase moves to the other end of the couch. He lifts my feet and puts them on his lap as he sits down. "That day," he says, wiping his hands over his face. "I've never told you everything about that day. I don't think you really want to know."

"Tell me, Chase. I need to know. Tell me. Please."

He sighs and looks away from me. "We were clearing a little Iraqi village. Mack peeled off for some reason and went into one of the buildings we were passing. I saw him go in. The building blew maybe twenty seconds later. There's no way he survived it. All of a sudden, we're taking enemy fire. We knew Mack was gone. The entire building was reduced to rubble—and him with it. I had to call for an immediate evacuation. A marine unit went in later that day to clear the site. They searched the entire area. There was nothing there. The explosion caused a fire. Everything was gone, Millie. Your dad was gone. He died instantly in the explosion."

I put my face in my hands and mumble through my fingers, "If you never recovered his body, whose ashes did we dump in the ocean?"

"I'm sorry, Millie. We had to give you something—something to lay to rest." Chase looks at me—his eyes pleading with me to understand. "They were ashes from a wood fire. Not human remains—not Mack. But he's dead, Millie. One hundred percent. He's dead."

"George said Dad faked his own death. That Yusef Hadzic had started looking for me. Dad wanted to disappear so he would stop looking. If Yusef couldn't find Dad, he couldn't find me."

Chase squints at me as he processes what I said. "Tell me again who George is."

"His name is George Chapman. He was my boss at the agency."

His eyes pop wide open. "Chapman is his last name? George Chapman?"

"Yeah. Why?"

"Tall, skinny guy? Black hair with glasses?"

"Yeah," I say, confused. "Do you know him?"

Chase lets out a long sigh. "Millie, George Chapman was the agency liaison for the SEAL teams when your dad and I were active."

"What do you mean? Like after Dad died? I don't think George knew him."

"He knew him. Really well. He was like that Raine woman is to Mason and his team. He worked with us daily."

"I've talked to George about Dad a lot. He's never once told me he knew him. That can't be right."

Chase stares straight ahead for a few minutes and then turns slowly to look at me. "Call Mason and get him over here. There's something happening that I don't like. We need him in on this conversation."

"Do you think Dad is alive?" I say, my eyes starting to tear up again.

Chase squeezes my feet. "He's not alive. I don't know what George is playing at here, but Mack isn't alive. I'm sorry, sweetie. Call Mason. Okay?"

Chapter Thirteen

MASON, SAN DIEGO, CALIFORNIA, 2020

It's been three hours since Millie left to go jogging. I'm about to go out of my mind. I haven't heard from her. I haven't called her. I'm trying to be patient. I'm trying not to worry. But three hours is enough to test anyone's limits, and I'm not anyone.

I learned in training that any deviation from the norm— even a small one—is reason for concern. Millie's never gone more than an hour when she jogs. I'm just about to track her phone when my phone rings. It's her. The worst-case scenarios run through my head as I answer it.

"Millie," I say, trying to keep the panic out of my voice. "Hey. Where are you? Are you okay?"

"Yeah, I'm fine. Sorry I've been gone so long." Her voice sounds shaky. "I'm at Chase's. Will you come over here?"

"I'll be there in two minutes," I say as I grab my car keys. I'm already out the front door before she can reply.

"Mase, I'm okay. Really." I can tell she's starting to cry.

"I know you are, babe. I'm almost there. I'm already on the freeway. Stay on the phone."

She doesn't say anything else, but I can hear her breathing. Honestly, that's enough for me right now.

I make it to Chase's in record time and find her pacing on his driveway with the phone still to her ear. I jump out of the car and run to hug her. She's shaking. I push her back a little bit to look at her. She's wearing one of Chase's big SEAL sweatshirts.

"Mills, what's going on?" I say cautiously. "I'm worried about you."

"Let's go inside. Chase wants to be in on the conversation, too."

I grab her by the arm and turn her to look at me. "Are you and Chase," I say, stumbling over my words, "together?"

The mere thought of it makes me want to kill someone—preferably Chase. I know in my heart it's not true, but here she stands in only his sweatshirt—not wearing anything she left the house in this morning. She's barefooted and her hair is that messy wild that only happens after she's been in bed.

It takes her a second to register what I said. "No. Mase. No. God no. It's about my dad. Just come inside."

She takes my hand and leads me inside. I see Chase sitting in his recliner, looking like someone sucked every bit of air out of his body. There are broken pieces of glass all over the floor, and as I get closer, I see almonds mixed in with the glass.

"What happened here?" I say, pulling back on Millie's hand, so she won't cut her feet.

"I dropped a jar of almonds." She lets go of my hand and tip toes around the glass and over to the couch.

"Is someone going to clean this up?" I'm so confused right now. Chase looks like he's going to pass out. Millie's crawling back into the spot where it looks like she's been sleeping—the pillows are fluffed up behind her and a blanket on top of her.

I walk straight through the mess—my flip-flops crunching through the debris—and plop down on the couch. Millie and Chase stare at each other. I'm getting nervous again.

"Someone say something!" My voice finally mirrors the anger that's taken over my body. "Now!"

"The agency thinks my dad could still be alive," Millie blurts out and then sinks under the blanket. All I can see is the top of her head. I turn to look at Chase.

"Don't look at me, man," he says, shaking his head. "I've told her they're completely full of shit."

I turn back around to Millie, who's still hiding under the blanket. "Millie. Look at me." She looks up slowly. "Your dad is not alive. And I didn't hear your boss say that when he was at the house."

"I met with him after he left the house. I wasn't going jogging. He had more to tell me."

"Millie," I say, frustrated, "come on. I thought we were past you hiding stuff from me. You promised."

"He wasn't going to tell me everything with you there, so I met with him separately. And I'm telling you now."

"Tell me everything." I slump down on the couch, resting my head on the back and closing my eyes. I need to mentally prepare for this.

"George says Dad faked his own death to prevent my

family from finding me. The Azayiz woman he was talking about this morning—my great-aunt—asked the agency to help him disappear after she found out Yusef Hadzic was looking for me. The agency thinks she might know where Dad is. And now she's missing."

"Millie," I say, opening my eyes, "that's a lot of bullshit. I know you want it to be true, but this George guy is trying to manipulate you into coming back. He knows if you have any hope your dad is still alive, you will stop at nothing to find him. He just wants you back working for him. That was pretty obvious this morning."

"Exactly what I said," Chase chimes in from across the room. "One weird thing, though. I just found out this George is the same George who was the agency strap to our team. He knew Mack really well. He never told Millie that."

My muscles start to tense up quickly. I look at Millie. "That just means he's been manipulating you for years instead of hours."

Millie tilts her head and raises her eyebrows—her warning look before she's about to get pissed about something. I saw it many times on our first mission together. She turns from me to Chase.

"George told me something else," she says slowly. "Azayiz is the informant credited with locating bin Laden. She was acquainted with his courier—the one they followed to his compound in Abbottabad. She knew his family growing up. They were both Pashtun from around where the FATA is now. She told the agency the courier worked for bin Laden. It's what eventually led to the raid."

Chase stops breathing. I immediately know from the look

in his eyes that his team was part of the UBL mission. For their own safety, the identities of those operators have been a closely held secret—even from those of us on the teams. But looking at him now, there's no doubt in my mind that he was there—which likely means Millie's dad was there, too.

Chase's eyes narrow. "What else did he tell you, Millie?"

"That Dad was on the UBL mission, too."

Before she can say anything more, Chase stands up abruptly.

"Here's what's going to happen," he says, suddenly looking like he's back at the lead of his team. "Is George still in town, Millie?'

"No. He was leaving for the airport when he left me. He's probably on his way back to DC by now. He's hoping I will join him tomorrow."

"If you go, I'm going with you," I say.

"Nope. Nope," Chase says. "You're staying here for now. You have a job, and BUD/S is going into Hell Week. You can't go AWOL. And besides, this is between George and me. I've got a lot I need to say to him, and it's not going to be pretty."

"If she's going to Pakistan," I say, growling at Chase, "I'm going with her."

"No one is going to Pakistan. Millie and I will go to D.C. tomorrow and have it out with George. We'll call you when we know more. Like we both said, this is just some bullshit fantasy to get her to rejoin the agency. No one is going to Pakistan."

"There's no way I'm staying here. Culver wants me to take back the lead of my team. I'll do that if I have to, but I'm not carrying on like nothing's happening."

"Mase," Millie says as she reaches for my hand, "I don't even know if I'm going to get to Virginia Beach. I might only be in D.C. for a few days and then back here. If you go, you're in for three or four months at least. Right?"

"Yeah, but it sounds like this one is going to get pushed through. One of the teams is going to be attached to this mission. I'd rather it be my team, with me at the lead."

"Yeah, but even if that's the case, there's no way Culver's going to assign your team. He knows about us," Millie says. "It's a huge professional conflict of interest."

"Millie, if you're going to Pakistan, I'm going with you. Not negotiable. I'll get Culver to agree to it."

"Honestly, I think he would prefer Mason and his team. They've worked with you already. And as far as your relationship goes, it's not like you're the first agency liaison to sleep with one of the operators," Chase says. He quickly adds, "Not that you two are just sleeping together, but you know what I mean."

"Mase," Millie says, "please give us twenty-four hours before you commit to four months. Okay? We'll call you tomorrow night. Nothing's going to happen in a day."

Chapter Fourteen

The second Mack walked into his office, George knew his day was going to get complicated. In the two years George had been the CIA liaison to the SEAL teams in Virginia Beach, Mack hadn't said two words to him—much less actively sought him out. But now Mack was sitting across the desk— his massive arms crossed rigidly in front of him.

"Mack," George said cautiously, "is there something I can do for you?'

Mack didn't say anything. He just sat there—his eyes fixed on George in a cold, unblinking stare. George began to shift uncomfortably in his chair.

"Mack," he tried again, "is there something wrong?"

"I need to disappear for a while," Mack said gruffly.

George's eyes narrowed into slits. "I don't know what that means."

"Disappear. You know what disappear means. Don't you

do stuff like that? The agency. Can't you make people disappear?"

George slowly reached for his phone. "Maybe we should get Chase in here. I think your team leader should be involved in this conversation."

"Put the phone down or you're going to lose that hand."

George dropped the phone immediately. Mack's face had turned from merely serious to downright deadly.

"Let's back up," George said, trying to relax into his chair. "Why do you need to disappear?'

"Do you know who Sayid Custovic is?"

"Of course I know who he is, Mack. He's one of the most-wanted terrorists in the world."

"He's also my daughter's uncle."

George froze. "What do you mean he's your daughter's uncle?" he said slowly.

"Uncle. Do you not know what that means either?" Mack pushed his arms across George's desk. "I hooked up with a Bosnian woman when we were assigned there in the nineties. Her name was Nejra Custovic. She was Sayid's sister. She had my baby. After she died, I got the baby. My daughter is Sayid's niece. You understand now?"

George tried to loosen his grip on the arms of his chair. "What are you talking about? This sounds crazy. Are you sure? Does anyone else know?"

"I know it sounds crazy, but it's true. Only a few people know. A few of Nejra's friends and family helped me get Millie out of Bosnia. I'm not going to go into how all that happened, but no one has ever tried to contact me or her in the sixteen years since I took her—until last night." Mack slammed his back against his chair, causing it to crash noisily into the wall.

"What happened last night?" George started shifting in his chair again.

"I had a visitor. One of Nejra's friends from Bosnia. He told me Sayid's lieutenant, Yusef Hadzic, was looking for me —for Millie."

"Who's the friend?"

"It doesn't matter. He's not involved in anything illegal. He came here just to warn me."

George took an extended breath and exhaled it forcefully through his mouth. "Mack, I'm not sure what you want me to do here. The agency doesn't really hide U.S. citizens. That's more of an FBI thing. And then it's really only for federal witnesses."

"Do you know who Azayiz Custovic is? The agency has her in protective custody in Pakistan. She's Millie's aunt. She sent the friend to me last night. Ask her if I'm telling you the truth."

George's eyes widened as he pushed his chair away from the desk. "Who told you we have Azayiz Custovic in protective custody? You're wading into really dangerous waters right now. I think maybe you should quit talking."

"Call your bosses. Tell them what I said. Tell them I know about Azayiz. The only thing that matters to me right now is protecting Millie. I will die to protect her. Or disappear. Or go to jail. Whatever it takes. I need for you to help me get them off Millie's trail."

George stood up. "I need to share this with my boss. If what you've said is true, we have a very delicate situation on our hands. I'm assuming you didn't ask permission before you took your daughter out of Bosnia. And that's just our first problem. The other bigger problem, of course, is that this now involves one of our most valuable informants. This is a lot to process. And we're wheels up to Iraq in a few days. You need to give me at least a week. I'll have to get back to you."

Mack walked over to George until he was standing inches from his face. "You have a day. Twenty-four hours. Figure it out. You have no idea what I will do to protect my daughter. I'll take down this entire operation if I have to—and you with it. One day."

As Mack slammed the door behind him, George quickly called his supervisor in D.C. "Paul, we've got a big problem. It involves Azayiz Custovic. And we've only got a day to fix it."

Chapter Fifteen

MILLIE, WASHINGTON, D.C., 2020

"Is your boyfriend hiding behind the door, waiting to attack me?" George says as I motion him into my hotel room.

"Nope."

He takes a small, slow step in—his eyes darting around the room.

"Are you going to come in?" I let the door fall against him as I walk over to the table. "Or do you want to meet in the hallway?"

"I find it very suspicious you didn't want to meet at the office," he says as he finally walks in. "But fine."

He's abruptly cut off by Chase slamming him against the wall. "Hi, George," Chase says in a menacing tone I've never heard from him before. "Long time, buddy."

George whips his head around to look at me—equal amounts of betrayal and anger shooting from his eyes.

"He's not my boyfriend," I say, glaring back at him. "And technically, he wasn't hiding behind the door."

George looks back at Chase. "I can explain."

"Doubtful." Chase flings him across the room toward the table. "Sit."

George reluctantly sits opposite of me. "I guess she told you," he says without looking at me.

"That you told her Mack was still alive. Yeah. She definitely told me that."

"I believe I asked you not to tell anyone," George says as he slowly turns to me.

"I don't work for you anymore. I don't work for the agency. I'll tell anyone anything."

"That's dangerous talk, Millie," George says, his voice shaking.

Chase comes over and kicks George's chair. "Your problem isn't with her. It's with me. And things are about to turn real dangerous if you don't start talking right now."

George shakes his head as he looks up at the ceiling. "I could get fired for this. Or worse."

"Believe me, the agency is the least of your worries," Chase growls. "Talk. Why did you tell her Mack is still alive?"

"I didn't tell her Mack was still alive," George says slowly.

"Bullshit!" Chase kicks his chair again.

George looks at me. "I didn't tell you he was still alive. I said there was a possibility. I don't know if he's alive."

"Enough with the semantics. Why do you think he wasn't killed that day in Iraq? You were in the control center when it happened. You saw the building go up. What makes you think he survived that?"

George looks down at his feet and whispers, "A tunnel. He escaped through a tunnel."

"What the hell are you talking about?" Chase paces across the room.

"Mack asked me not to tell you," George says. "I wanted to. Actually, let me be crystal clear. He demanded I not tell you. He threatened me. You know how he was. I thought he was going to kill me."

"He asked you not to tell me what?" Chase says through his tightly clenched teeth.

"That he wanted to disappear. That he was afraid Millie's life was in danger and he wanted to fake his own death to protect her."

"Let me get this straight. You're claiming Mack came to you and asked you to help him disappear," Chase says. "That's insane. Mack would never do that."

"He did it. He came to my office. Told me he had been approached by a friend of Millie's mother. The friend told him Yusef Hadzic was looking for Millie to use her as bait to pull Azayiz Custovic out of hiding." George takes a deep breath and turns to look out the window. "And we did it."

"He never would have done that without telling me. Never," Chase says.

"If he told you, would you have helped him?" George looks at the expression on Chase's face. "Exactly. That's why he didn't tell you. You never would have agreed to it."

"I never would have agreed to it because it's the craziest, stupidest idea I've ever heard. And I still don't think Mack asked you to do shit for him. You're making this up so Millie will think he's alive, and it will give her incentive to come back to the agency. And that really does make me want to kill you."

George shrinks back in his chair as Chase walks toward him again.

"Prove it," I blurt out.

"What?" George looks from Chase back to me.

"Prove it. If you helped my dad disappear, prove it. Where is he? Surely the agency has kept in touch with him. I mean you supposedly helped a Navy SEAL fake his own death and put him into hiding. Prove it. Tell us where he is."

George stares at me for a minute and then looks back up at the ceiling—shaking his head.

"When Mack left my office that day, I called my supervisor in D.C. immediately. After I told him what was happening, he told me he would call me back. He called me back in less than five minutes and told me he was handling it from that point forward. He told me to keep my mouth shut and continue on as if nothing had happened. The next day, I saw Mack being pulled into a meeting with navy brass."

"I saw that, too," Chase says. "Mack told me it was about his retirement."

"C'mon, Chase. How many SEALs get that level of brass to attend their retirement meeting?" George turns briefly to look at me. I think he senses I'm starting to put all of the pieces together.

"I thought it was because he was the first one of us from *that* mission to retire. Maybe it required extra safety protocols or something," Chase says, shaking his head. I can tell he's starting to figure it out, too.

"Did the brass come in for your retirement? You were the

team leader. You knew more than anyone. Did they come in for you?"

Chase sits on the bed. "What happened next?" he says, looking down.

George continues. "The next thing I heard from my boss was a couple days later when we were headed to Iraq. He told me to brief your team on the raid where Mack died, or more accurately, where he disappeared. The information I gave you on the village that day was fake. There were no insurgents anywhere close to that area. I told my boss that it was false information. He told me again to keep my mouth shut and give the information to you. When the building blew and you started receiving fire, I didn't know any of that was going to happen. But the way it went down—with everything that had just happened with Mack—I knew immediately when you called in his death that there was more to the story."

"I remember the enemy fire wasn't hitting that close to us that day. I just thought they were bad shots," Chase says. "And they were all shooting from one area. They had the high ground on us. If they would have fanned out, we would have been sitting ducks. I always thought we got lucky."

"I'm assuming we were running that enemy fire to get you to call for an evacuation, so you wouldn't poke around the house looking for Mack's remains. I don't know, though. I was told to stay in my lane, and I did. I didn't ask any questions after it happened. All I know is that I was given a promotion soon after that and moved to D.C." George looks back at me. "I put it behind me until five years later when the CIA director came to my office personally and told me that Mack's daughter just completed training at Langley. He said she was being assigned to me and that I had two directives regarding her: Keep her away from Sayid Custovic's network and don't tell her anything about my association with Mack."

I feel like I'm going to pass out. I put my head in my hands to try to stop the spinning.

"George, how could you keep this from me?" I ask without looking up. "All these years. You know how much my dad's death devastated me. You thought there was some chance he was alive and you didn't even mention it to me?"

"Millie, I'm sorry, but this isn't personal. If there's one thing you know about me, it's that I'm a company man. I was told what to do, and I did it. I'm not a free spirit like you. I do what I'm told. I wish you weren't finding this out at all because it's getting your hopes up again. I really don't know if he's alive. When Azayiz went missing, the director told me to get you back in the fold. You wouldn't come back, so he told me to tell you that your dad might still be alive and that Azayiz would know."

"So is that a lie?" I look up at him. "That my dad is alive?"

"I really don't know, Millie. I suspect we helped him disappear that day. I suspect Azayiz had some involvement in it. But beyond that, I don't know."

"Mills." Chase squats down in front of my chair and takes my hands. "Let's go home. It's not worth it. It's been nine years. Even if he was alive that day, he's probably not now. He would have contacted you. Or me. Let's just go home."

I look at him for a minute and then turn to George. "I want to meet with the director."

"Millie," George says quietly.

"No, George. If you want me to go to Pakistan, I meet with him first. If not, Chase and I will go home."

"I don't know that I can make that happen." George stands up and looks at Chase for permission before he starts walking to the door.

"That's up to you—to the agency—but if you want me back in, I talk to the director. Final word."

George nods as he walks out the door. "I'll call you later today."

Chapter Sixteen

MILLIE, WASHINGTON, D.C., 2020

"He's not coming with us," Ted says, pointing at Chase.

The agency director granted my request for a meeting about an hour after George left my room. George's driver, Ted, arrived at our hotel soon after to take me to the meeting.

Chase puts his arm around my shoulders.

"I'm not going without him, Ted. And this time, I don't think you're going to be able to force me into the car," I say, smiling at him.

"My instructions are to bring you—just you," he says, eyeing Chase. Ted's a tough guy, but from the drawn look on his face, I don't think he wants any part of Chase. Probably a smart decision. Chase's anger level has been steadily rising since we left San Diego.

Finally, Ted nods his head and motions us toward the car. Chase pulls me back and looks in the car before I get in. Seeing that there's no one already in there, he helps me in— blocking me from taking Ted's outstretched hand.

As Ted closes the door, Chase says, "I'm going all the way to the director's office with you."

"Shh," I whisper, pointing to the speakers behind our heads. Every agency car is equipped with them. The microphones inside can supposedly be turned off at the rider's request. I've always assumed they're on and someone's listening. Frankly, I'd be disappointed if they weren't spying on their own people. Every agent I know keeps more from their bosses than they tell them. We ride in silence the rest of the way.

One of the director's assistants meets us at the car. I make it clear to him that Chase is coming with me wherever I go. He vehemently disagrees. We finally negotiate that Chase can come to the outer area of the director's office, but not inside. They must really be desperate to find Azayiz because no one has this kind of negotiating power in the agency. I keep asking, and much to my surprise, they keep saying yes. It's all making me very suspicious.

"Wait here," the assistant says to Chase as we get off the elevator on the executive level.

Chase looks from him to me. "You okay?"

"Yeah, I'm good," I say, patting him on the arm.

We go through a series of doors that lead to the director's office. The assistant nods at the final level of security. They open the door for me. I look back at the assistant, who motions me to go in without him. I walk into the massive office slowly.

"I knew you were going to be an inconvenience one day." I hear a man's voice coming from the far corner of the room. I look over and see Paul Ward, the agency's director, sitting in a chair against the wall. He motions me to take the chair opposite him.

"Is that what I am? An inconvenience?" I say as I walk over to him. "I'm sorry if me putting an end to the Custovic network—after you tried to do it unsuccessfully for nearly two decades—was an inconvenience."

He stares at me with an amused look in his eyes. "Actually, we prefer our agents don't get kidnapped in the pursuit of our goals."

"Means to an end," I say as I sit down. "They're dead, aren't they? A simple thank you would suffice."

He shakes his head as a smile starts forming at the corners of his mouth. "Well, you're as arrogant as your dad. That's for sure."

"Thank you. Now can the small talk end? Is my dad alive?"

His smile flatlines. He stares at me for a good minute. I don't think he blinks once.

Finally he says, "Would you believe me if I told you I didn't know?"

"Tell me what you do know."

"You don't have the clearance for it and you know that."

"Look, how important is Azayiz to you? And how necessary am I in the mission to retrieve her? That's what it boils down to. If you want me to help you find her, I need answers first."

"Retrieving her is of vital importance," he says, pausing for a second. "And the agent in charge is convinced that dangling you out as bait is the best way to do that. I would rather you not be involved, but here we are."

"Then start talking."

"Show some respect, Agent Marsh."

"Respect works both ways, Director Ward."

He glares at me. I return it right back to him. No one says anything for an uncomfortably long time.

"This doesn't leave this room," he commands. "If you tell anyone—including your little bodyguard out in the lobby—I will lock you up and leave you there. Do you understand?"

I nod. He takes a deep breath and stares at me for another few seconds before he starts in.

"As you might know from your pursuit of him, Yusef Hadzic had ties to Al Qaeda. He wanted to merge your uncle's network with them. Your uncle Sayid apparently didn't want that. He had no problem working with them, but he wanted to retain his autonomy. Sayid and Yusef had a power struggle for years. Yusef had a slight advantage with his Al Qaeda alliance. When we took out UBL, Yusef's advantage disappeared immediately. We didn't know any of this until after they died. Sayid kept extensive journals. The operators recovered them on the day they rescued you."

He pauses to pour himself a cup of coffee. He motions to the cup in front of me. I shake my head. The last thing I need right now is more stimulation. My head is already buzzing. He takes a long sip of coffee and continues.

"Azayiz's son, Fareed, was part of the network, too. He was a strong supporter of Sayid, but didn't have much love for Yusef. He was passing information to his mother about the network. Most of it seemed targeted at taking Yusef out of the equation, although we didn't fully understand that until recently. I believe George told you Azayiz was instrumental in the tip that led us to find bin Laden's courier. That information came from Fareed. We now think Sayid wanted that information passed to us. When UBL died, it stripped Yusef of all his power. Yusef was pissed as you can imagine. He couldn't touch Fareed without dying himself, so he set his sights on Azayiz. Fareed found out and told her. That's when we rushed her into hiding. The amount of information that woman knows is staggering. If our enemies get her, it would be devastating to our operations in that region. Frankly, right now, the best-case scenario is that they find her and kill her immediately."

"Okay. So I understand why she's so valuable, but what does this have to do with my dad?" I say. "He's the only reason I'm here."

"I was in charge of Middle Eastern operations in 2011 when this all went down. Azayiz was my responsibility. That day—when George called me and told me what your dad said —I saw my entire operation falling apart. One of our special forces guys had a daughter whose uncle was Sayid Custovic. It doesn't get any worse than that. And then factor in that your dad was one of the operators on the bin Laden mission, and he knows we have Azayiz in hiding, and he's threatening to expose all of that if we don't help him go into hiding. It was the worst-case scenario. No offense, but my life would have been a whole lot easier if you had never been born."

"No offense taken. I could probably say the same about you."

"Bottom line, I told Azayiz about your dad's request to go into hiding. She told me she had initiated it. Frankly, I wanted to kill both of them. All of this to protect one girl. It pissed me off. But unfortunately, I couldn't kill anyone, so I made a deal with them. We would help your dad fake his death, but then we were out. He only had to agree to never surface again. And to never enter back into this country. I worked out the deal with the agency and the navy. We eliminated him from naval records and took away his passport. As far as we were concerned, he was dead."

"But was he? George said there was a tunnel underneath the house that blew up. Do we even know he made it into the tunnel?"

"Yeah, he made it in. We had agents waiting for him. When they had him in the tunnel, they detonated the explosives that blew the house. We took him to Baghdad, and that was it."

"You just left him in Baghdad? I don't think I believe that."

"Azayiz had someone meet our agents there. They took him. I don't know who they were. I didn't want to know. Like I said, after the house blew, he was dead to us."

"So you handed him over to some guys who could have very well killed him that day?"

"We handed him off to who Azayiz instructed us to hand him off to. We didn't do this for your dad. We're not in the business of making members of our military disappear. I wouldn't have even considered it if he didn't play the Azayiz card. Bluntly, she was—and still is—much more important to us than your dad. I'm sorry if that hurts your feelings."

"It doesn't hurt my feelings. I used the agency as a way to find out who my mom was. It's why I joined, and it's why I quit after I accomplished that. I have no interest in this agency beyond that."

"So I'm guessing you're not going to help us find Azayiz then?"

"I didn't say that. She was the one who told my dad to rescue me as a baby. I don't know what she's become now, but I owe her my life for that. And if you're telling the truth—which I think you are—then she's the only one who would know what happened to Dad after the tunnel. I have to at least try to find out. I'll go to Pakistan on one condition."

"I think this entire conversation has been enough of a condition. You don't have any more favors stored up."

"Maybe not, but I'm going to ask anyway. My bodyguard —as you call him—was my dad's team leader."

"I know who he is."

"When I leave for Pakistan, I want the agency to arrange for him to go back to Iraq and try to retrace my dad's steps from that side. And I want you to send Raine Laghari with him."

"The agent assigned to the teams in Virginia Beach? Why her?"

"Because she's the only person I trust in the agency."

"You don't trust George?"

"Not at all. And I definitely don't trust you."

He smiles. "I'm okay with sending them over there, but Millie, best-case scenario that your dad is alive, he agreed to never surface and never come back to this country. If you find him, what then?"

"One step at a time," I say, standing up. "I don't get on a plane until Raine and Chase tell me they're on their way to Iraq."

He nods. "Agent Marsh."

I turn back around to face him.

"I hope you find what you're looking for. Surprisingly, I kind of like you."

I stare at him for a second and leave without replying.

Chase and I ride back to the hotel in silence. Once we get there, I make him stand outside by the loud fountains as I tell him everything the director told me. He doesn't say anything until I'm done talking.

Finally he takes a deep breath and says, "Are you okay? That's the most important thing to me right now."

"Yeah. It's a lot, but I'm fine. I think he's telling the truth."

"You're better at reading people than I am, so let's assume he is. It still doesn't mean Mack's alive. But let's find out—put this bullshit to rest once and for all." He pulls me to him and hugs me tightly. "Promise me you won't get your hopes up. Swear to me."

I rest my head on his chest and hug him back. "I promise. Let's get this over with and get back home."

"Agreed," he says. "Are you okay if I go back to my room? I need to call Mariel, and it's not going to be pretty."

"Yeah. I'm good."

"And you're going to call Mason?"

"Yeah, I'll call you after I talk to him."

When I get to my room, I place the call. He answers on the first ring.

"Well, Millie Marsh," Captain Culver says. "To what do I owe this pleasure?"

"Hey, Captain. I think I'm going to be seeing you soon."

"I hope for personal reasons, but from the tone of your voice, I'm guessing it's for other reasons."

"Yeah. I can't talk about it on an unsecured line. But, yeah, I'm sure you'll hear about it in the next few hours. In the meantime, I need to ask you a favor."

"Anything," he says. "You know that."

"This mission is going to make Mason want to come back as team lead—"

"Millie," he interrupts, "don't even ask me to say no to him. I need him here, and that's not within your purview to ask."

"No, it's not that," I say slowly. "But I don't want him on this mission. You know we're dating. It would be a huge conflict of interest. Neither one of us could be objective. Will you promise me that?"

Chapter Seventeen

MASON, SAN DIEGO, CALIFORNIA, 2020

When I hang up the phone with Millie, I'm mad. I know she's not telling me everything. Again. But at least she told me she's going to Pakistan. And that means I'm going, too. I call Culver.

"I've been waiting for your call," Culver says. "I just got the brief on the new mission involving Millie."

"Yeah. I have to be in on that one."

"Look, Mason. I want you back. You know that. But if you come back, you're in for three or four months—however long it takes Stevie to recover. And, of course, I'll take you longer than that—however long you want to stay."

"Yeah. I get it. I'm in—for as long as it takes."

"And just because you're coming back doesn't mean you're going on this mission. It sounds like we're going in immediately on this one, and I'm not sure you're going to be mission-ready by then."

"Give me any test you want to give me. I haven't lost a step. I'm ready right now."

"I'm sure that's true. Just get here, and we can talk about it then. I'll set you up with transport out this afternoon. Get to the base as soon as possible."

When I get on the plane, I call Millie for the third time. I haven't talked to her since she called me this morning. She's not answering my calls or the several texts I've sent.

Unfortunately, I find out why when I land in Virginia Beach. Culver meets my plane. I'm barely on firm ground when he starts in.

"Millie asked me not to put your team on this mission."

The engines are still winding down on the plane, so I think —and hope—I misunderstood him. "What'd you say?"

"You heard me the first time. She thinks it's a conflict of interest because you're dating," he says with annoyance rising in his voice. "Why didn't you leave her alone when I asked you to? I knew something like this was going to happen."

I want to punch something so badly right now, but I know I need to keep everything in check, including my tone. "You're not considering sending someone else, are you?" I say as unemotionally as I can. "You know my team is the best positioned for this mission."

"I know, and it pisses me off that something else is clouding my decision. I don't like emotional decisions, and I'm starting to feel like this is one," he snarls.

"It's not for me," I continue on in an impressively even tone, considering how mad I am. Culver pulled me off the mission where she was kidnapped. I can't let someone be responsible for her safety again. "This is not personal. My team's the most qualified. We're already read in on the details of this network—this family. We've worked with Millie. The minute this mission starts, it's one hundred percent about the job for me—and it will be for her, too. I guarantee that."

We've reached the parking lot where JJ—my second-in-command on the team—is waiting for me.

"Let me think about it," Culver says as he heads to his car. "I'll call you later tonight."

"Welcome back, brother," JJ says, cautiously eyeing my clenched jaw. He knows how to read every one of my moods, and he knows this one isn't good. "What's Culver thinking about?"

"Millie asked him to call us off this mission," I say as I throw my backpack into the back seat.

"She did what now?" JJ shakes his head—the way he does when he disagrees with me on a decision I make on a mission.

"You heard me."

"You talk to her about it?"

"Not yet," I say, slamming the door so hard, it makes the car vibrate for a second. "She's not returning my messages."

JJ whistles. "Whew. How's that sitting with you?"

"Not well," I say, pounding my fist into the dashboard. "Not well at all. I'm going to need several shots of whiskey in my system right now."

"Good thing we're headed to a bar then."

"Don't tell any of the other guys about Millie. Just between us."

JJ nods. "I know this is the wrong time to talk about it, but when this is over, I think you seriously need to reevaluate your relationship. I told you from the beginning you were stepping on a land mine with that one."

"You're right. It's not the time to talk about it, but it's definitely entered my mind more than a few times today," I say as we pull into the bar parking lot. "By the way, sorry about that dent I put in your dashboard."

As soon as we walk in the door, the jaw jacking starts hitting me from all sides.

"Well look what the cat drug in," Butch drawls as he points his pool stick at me. "We got a California boy in our presence."

I give him a harder than necessary chest bump. "Man, you know this blood is all Texas. That California air isn't strong enough to change that."

Hawk comes over and shoves me from behind. "I don't know, man. Your hair is looking real pretty. You getting Hollywood on us?"

"I live in San Diego, dumbass," I say as I duck to avoid his attempt at messing up my hair.

"What's up, Bryce?" I say to the rookie of the group. "Man, you leave for a couple months and your kids are full-grown when you get back. You almost have a real man's beard now."

"Ah no, that's still just baby peach fuzz," Ty says as he tugs on Bryce's beard on the way over to me. "Good to see you, brother. You've been missed."

I chuck him on the shoulder. "Damn. I hate to admit it, but I missed your ugly faces, too. Where's Mouse? He hiding in a corner somewhere as usual?"

They all start laughing, shaking their heads. "Mouse has

got himself a lady friend since you've been gone," Butch says. "And she's got him on a short leash—barely lets him poke his head outside when we're in town."

"Speaking of leashes, did Millie give you permission to leave town?" Hawk says. "Or did she finally come to her senses and break up with your ugly ass?"

"Are we going to talk about relationships and then braid each other's hair?" JJ steps in. "Let's play pool. Butch and Mase owe me at least five thousand dollars in losses, and tonight's my night to get it back."

"Never going to happen, brother," I say, patting him on the back.

Butch hands me a pool stick. "You still got any skill, or am I going to have to find another partner?"

I shove him toward the head of the table. "Just shut up and break."

As I watch him break, I get a text from Culver.

You're in. Meeting at seven hundred tomorrow morning. Wheels up likely tomorrow afternoon. Welcome back.

Chapter Eighteen

"Mack, I'm sorry," Rear Admiral Peters said. "This is the only way we will even consider doing this for you. If you leave, you're gone for good."

Mack started to protest again, but Peters cut him off.

"Frankly, I wouldn't even be considering this at all if our partners at the agency weren't asking," Peters continued. "I can't believe you kept this information from us. Do you have any idea the risk you put your team in? Your daughter's related to one of the most dangerous terrorists in the world. It's such a conflict to have you on the teams. I would have dismissed you on the spot if I had known—or locked you up. But I'm guessing you knew that."

"I didn't tell anyone for my daughter's safety. It wasn't about keeping my job," Mack said. "Her safety's the only thing that has ever mattered to me."

"And how's that working out for you now? If we're to believe the agency, Yusef Hadzic is tracking you and your daughter. And I'm truly sorry for both of you. But my job is to protect the teams, and you being part of them is a huge safety breach for the program—not to mention the PR problems. If the press found out that one of our elite special operators is related to an international terrorist . . . it would be unbelievably damaging to our reputation."

Mack's chest tightened. He took a deep breath to try to remain calm. "I don't understand why I can't disappear until we take out their organization and then come back."

Peters' face remained hard. "We've been trying to find them for fifteen years, with absolutely no luck. If we ever find them—and that's a huge if—then possibly we would consider you coming back. But until then, if you disappear, we're wiping you clean—no passport, your citizenship revoked, wiped clean from naval records. We can't put ourselves in danger because of your secret."

Mack slowly nodded his head as he considered his choices.

"If you want to take your daughter with you, we'd consider delivering her to wherever you end up—"

Mack cut Peters off. "No. No way. She stays right where she is."

"We can't protect her, Mack. She'll get death benefits, so no one suspects anything, but we can't physically protect her. I'm sorry, but she's not our problem."

"I don't need you to protect her. I've got that covered."

"No active SEALs can help you with this. I'll ask you again: Do any of your team members know who she really is?"

"And I tell you again: no. No one knows."

"Not even Chase?"

"Chase doesn't know," Mack said, lying. Chase was the only person he had ever told about who Millie really was.

Peters folded his arms as he stared at Mack. "What's it going to be, Mack? I need your decision now."

"Let's do it," Mack said quietly. "I need to disappear."

Peters stood up. "It's going to happen on this trip to Iraq. Your agency contact will let you know the details as soon as we have them firmed up. Good luck to you, Mack."

Mack stood up and shook Peters's outstretched hand. "Thank you, sir."

When Mack left the office, he saw Chase standing to the side.

"What was that all about?" Chase said.

"Some bullshit about retirement," Mack said, avoiding Chase's eyes.

"They trying to talk you into staying?"

Mack started walking down the hall away from the office. "Naw. I guess I'm the first of the guys on the UBL mission to retire. They were just going over what's acceptable to say in the outside world and what's not."

"What's acceptable?"

"Basically nothing. Keep your mouth shut and forget it ever happened."

"Sounds about right. I'm retiring three months after you. I guess I'll get that talk soon."

"Probably," Mack said, changing the subject. "They found anyone to replace you at team lead?"

"Probably Bobby. He's been waiting for a team. I don't know, though. I'd give the keys to Harry right now."

"No, man. He's too young."

"I don't know. I think he's definitely going to make it further than any of us. Maybe Rear Admiral Culver someday."

Mack tried to play along, but his mind was on Millie. He wished he could see her one more time, but he knew he'd never be able to leave if he did. "Yeah, that'll be the day. No way Culver outranks you," Mack said, forcing a smile.

Chase grabbed Mack's arm and stopped him. "You okay? You seem kind of out of it."

"Yeah, I'm good. All good," Mack said briskly. "Just looking forward to getting over there. You know I get restless when we're not busy."

"Yeah, well wheels up tomorrow morning. Hopefully we'll get back soon, so it won't delay your trip to San Diego with Millie. When are you scheduled to leave? August 6?"

"That's the plan," Mack said, his voice cracking slightly.

Chase sighed. "Well you know what we always say: 'No plan survives first contact with the enemy.'"

Chapter Nineteen

MILLIE, VIRGINIA BEACH, VIRGINIA, 2020

When I drive past the guard gate at the base, I glance over to the last place I saw my dad alive. For the first time, it doesn't fill me with dread. I'm trying to keep my promise to Chase, but despite my best efforts to suppress it, I can feel a little glimmer of hope growing inside me.

I pull into the parking lot and see Raine waiting for me as usual. She's not even trying to control the smirk that's growing on her face.

"I knew you couldn't stay away from all of this," she says, sweeping her arm dramatically in the air like she's Vanna White introducing the next puzzle.

I grab her into a hug. "You said I couldn't stay away from the agency. The truth is I couldn't stay away from you."

"I knew it! That's the real reason you're having problems with Mason," she says, laughing.

"We're not really having problems. Just small stuff."

"He proposed to you, and you said no. That's not small

stuff. And I believe that's two guys who have made that mistake. Or am I forgetting someone?"

"You're not forgetting anyone, smartass," I say, flicking her on the shoulder. "And the two situations are completely different. The first was a definite no. This one is a—not now, but maybe later."

"I'm sure that made Mason feel so much better about it," she says, rolling her eyes. "And you cannot tell me if Alex hadn't been transferred to Moscow, you wouldn't be married to him right now and raising your gorgeous babies."

I shrug. "I guess we'll never know."

She pulls me to the side before we go into the building.

"I got a call from the director's office," she whispers. "They said you requested me on a mission to Iraq. I'm supposed to be briefed this afternoon. What's going on?"

"Let's talk about it after this meeting. It's about my dad. I need you to work on a recon mission with his friend Chase. You met him a few months ago when we got back from Bosnia."

She looks at me warily, but nods. We start back toward the situation room.

"So what's my new team like?" I say as we arrive at the door. "Which team did I get?"

She frowns. "What do you mean, your 'new team'?"

"I asked Culver to assign me a new team, so I wouldn't have to work with Mason. Who's my new team leader? Do I know him?"

She laughs and shakes her head. "Yeah, you know him."

She punches in the security code and swings the door

open. "You know what they say—everything old is new again."

As I walk through the door, I see Mason leaning against the wall—arms crossed defiantly in front of him—staring at me. He doesn't smile. He doesn't nod. He just glares at me with a look that could melt paint right off the wall.

"Hail. Hail. The gang's all here." I hear a Southern drawl so deep it has to be Butch. I turn toward the corner to see him grinning at me. "And I guess you thought you were rid of us. Surprise. Surprise."

I look around the room to see Mason's old team all staring at me with varying degrees of disdain and delight on their faces. They're all here—JJ, Bryce, Hawk, Ty, Mouse. JJ's glaring at me. I'm guessing he knows about my request to waive their team off this mission, which of course means Mason knows.

Captain Culver walks over to me. "Agent Marsh. Glad to have you back."

"Captain," I say quietly. "From the look on Mason's face, I'm guessing you told him about my request."

"I'm guessing I did."

"And do we really think that was necessary?"

"Yes we do. As I've told you before, my teams need to know everything before they take on a mission."

"I believe I asked you not to assign this team to this mission."

"You know I've always thought—over my thirty-plus years of doing this job—there was something missing from my decision-making process," he says, pausing dramatically.

"I'm so glad to finally realize that it was getting Millie Marsh's approval."

"Funny. Seriously. You missed your calling as a comedian," I say as I glance back over at Mason. "And I didn't say you needed my approval. I was asking you for a favor."

"And your favor has been denied. He's the best person for this mission. His team is the best. Stay in your lane, Agent Marsh."

"All righty then," I say as I start to walk away.

He grabs my shoulder and turns me back around. "Millie, Chase told me what's happening. I was there that day, too. Mack isn't alive. I want him to be for you—for all of us. He's not though. I'm so sorry, but he's not."

I stare at him blankly for a minute, but then nod. He pats me on the shoulder as he walks away. I look back to Mason, who hasn't moved a muscle. As discreetly as possible, I make my way across the room to him. He doesn't make any attempt at civility.

"Hey," I whisper.

He shakes his head in disgust. I stare back at him for a second, but as always, I know I'm not going to win a staring contest with him, so I try again. "Are you going to talk to me?"

"Yeah, I'll talk to you. How about this?" he hisses. "What the fuck, Millie? Were you going to tell me about this? Or are we back to you hiding secrets from me? That worked out so well last time. You told Culver not to let my team cover this? That's too fucking far, Millie. Way too far."

I keep my voice low and calm, trying to stay professional.

"Don't you think this is a conflict of interest? Your team covering me on this."

"It's a huge conflict of interest, which is how I know you're going to get back here safely," he says, the anger pouring out of his mouth like hot lava. "You want to lie to me? That's up to you. But if you're going to do this ludicrous thing, I'm going with you. Not a chance in hell I'm letting someone else be responsible after what happened last time."

"This kind of emotion is what I'm talking about. You're not being objective. That's the reason I wanted someone else."

"What did you say to me?" He uncrosses his arms and pushes himself off the wall. He gets inches from my face. "Did you say I'm too emotional to do my job?"

"That's not what I said," I say quickly.

"That's exactly what you said. You worry about your job. I'll take care of mine."

He takes a seat next to JJ at the table. They both stare at me—arms folded, eyes cold and hard. I'm trying to figure out how I'm going to fix this when I hear an enthusiastic "My girl Millie!" coming from the direction of the door. The voice sounds unsettlingly familiar—like a part of my past suddenly slapping me in the face. I look over to see my ex-boyfriend Alex walking over to me—his arms spread as wide as his smile.

Before I can even register what's happening, Alex surrounds me in a bear hug, burying my face against his chest. He holds me there for what is way too long to be professional. I'm so confused, I don't have the power to pull away. Finally he loosens his grip and pushes me back a little bit.

"Damn, girl, I don't look that much older, do I?" He smiles

widely again with that gleaming-white, perfectly straight grin that hypnotized me for most of my first year at the agency.

"What are you doing here?" I've finally found my voice. I take a few steps back from him.

"What do you mean? I'm here to work the op with you," he says, laughing. "Didn't George tell you?"

I look at Raine, who puts her hands up defensively and quickly walks away.

"No. He definitely didn't tell me you were part of this op."

"Well, I'm not just part of this op—I'm undercover as your husband," he says, hugging me again. "Perfect person for the job. Don't you think?"

Chapter Twenty

MASON, VIRGINIA BEACH, VIRGINIA, 2020

I take my seat at the table just as the door opens and some guy I've never seen walks in. He's dressed head to toe in black—black jeans, black button-up, black tailored jacket. He takes off his aviators and hangs them on his shirt as his eyes dart around the room. He seems to have found his target. I direct my eyes to where he's looking just as he says, "My girl Millie!"

The tone is way too flirty to be directed at her by anyone but me. I knew I didn't like him the second he walked in, and now I really don't like him. He walks over to Millie and pulls her into a hug. Millie doesn't make any effort to pull away. My body instinctively starts to rise. JJ puts his arm in front of me, blocking me from moving. I settle uncomfortably back into my seat, but my eyes don't budge off them. His hands are still on Millie's shoulders, and he's smiling at her with some bullshit fraternity-boy smile.

"Damn, girl. I don't look that much older, do I?" He

tousles her hair playfully as he takes a step back. After all these years, I'm finally starting to understand why they don't allow us to bring loaded weapons into this room.

Culver walks over to me. "His name is Alex Laskin. He's the lead agent on this mission. He's the new head of Middle Eastern operations. Not sure how he knows Millie."

I nod as I tune back into their conversation just in time to hear Alex say, "Well I'm not just part of this op—I'm undercover as your husband. Perfect person for the job. Don't you think?"

"What the fuck does that mean?" I say under my breath. JJ's arm starts to rise again. I shove it away.

"I know you're probably a little nervous about your first field assignment," Alex says, taking Millie's arm to lead her over to two open chairs opposite of us. "But don't worry, I'll teach you everything you need to know."

As he puts his hand intimately on the small of her back, I jump up, pushing my chair hard against the back wall. Hawk slides in front of me. "He's going to teach her how to be a field agent, not all the positions of the *Karma Sutra*. Settle down."

Butch rolls my chair back behind me, letting it hit the back of my knees as he tries to push my shoulders down. "I'm guessing Mason already taught her most of those positions. From what I hear, y'all been going at it like rabbits out there in San Diego."

"Shut up, Butch." I sit down, my eyes still firmly fixed across the room.

"Man, you have been gone too long if you think you can shut him up." Hawk laughs from behind me.

"Everybody settle in," Culver says as he walks to the front of the room. "I want to introduce you to Alex Laskin, who will be running point on this mission for the agency. He's been on the job for close to two decades—most of that in the field. He's been the head of the agency's Middle Eastern operations for a few months now. I'll let him fill you in on the rest."

Alex pushes his chair back and extends his legs out in front of him, like he's getting in a comfortable position to watch a football game. His entire posture pisses me off.

"Thanks, Captain," he starts. "I'll get right to it. Our target is Azayiz Custovic. She's a native of Pakistan, but also has Bosnian citizenship through marriage. She's been a CIA operative since 1995. She has been under our protective custody since 2011. She recently went missing from her safe house in Islamabad."

"What does 'missing' mean? Was she taken? Or did she leave on her own?" Bryce asks.

"Undetermined," Alex says. "There were no signs of struggle, but we can't think of a reason she would leave without telling us."

"Why was she under protective custody?" Ty asks.

"She's been informing on the Custovic/Hadzic network from day one. Her son, Fareed, was part of that network. We think he was feeding her information. She instantly became a target of the network—particularly of Yusef Hadzic. He's dead now, but he passed the information on to his associates over the years. Azayiz is one of the most-wanted people throughout the terrorist networks."

"Why would she run now? What's changed? Did someone

in the agency give away her location?" I ask, glaring at him. I can definitely see this douche being a double agent.

"Absolutely not." He spins around to face me. "No one gave up her location."

"It's essential to find out if she was kidnapped or left on her own. If she was taken by a terrorist group, she's probably dead. Have you had any ransom demands? Have there been any videos?" Culver says.

"Because we haven't had any of that, we think she's still alive," Alex says. "We're leaning toward her leaving on her own."

"Do we have any intel on where she might run to?" Butch asks.

"Limited," Alex says. "She has contacts all over Islamabad and Peshawar, where she was born. We're working those sources."

"So why are we going over now?" JJ says.

"Bluntly, our new strategy is to use Agent Marsh as bait. Azayiz is her great-aunt," Alex says as he puts his hand on her shoulder. It's way too intimate. I want to knock his hand off her shoulder and then knock his head clear off his body. "When Sayid Custovic died, we found a wealth of journals he kept throughout his life. Those journals lead us to believe Azayiz was particularly close to Agent Marsh's mother, Nejra. And that she was likely responsible for helping Agent Marsh's father locate Millie after her mother died."

"So the plan's to dangle Millie out as bait to get this woman to come out of hiding?" Butch says. "How exactly is that going to work?"

"Agent Marsh and I are getting married," Alex says, smiling broadly.

"You're doing what now?" I say, the anger rising in my voice.

"Fake married, of course." He smiles down at Millie, who I notice is not returning the smile. "Part of my job as the new head of Middle Eastern operations is to improve relations with the Pakistan government. I've been spending a lot of time there. I let it drop that I was getting married. They invited me to bring my wife to stay at the beautiful Serena Hotel in Islamabad. It's the perfect place for us to be right now. Azayiz worked at the hotel spa before we took her under protective custody. She still has contacts there. The news will get back to her that Nejra's daughter is in town on her honeymoon. We expect she'll move heaven and earth for a chance to see Millie."

"Honeymoon in Islamabad," Hawk says, shaking his head. "Bold choice."

"When did we decide this strategy?" All eyes—including mine—turn to Millie. Her tone's even enough to fool most of the room, but I'm definitely hearing the edge she gets when she's about to lose it on someone.

Alex turns toward her. "Did you and George not talk about this assignment? I was assuming he told you everything."

"We definitely talked," she says. "But I'm pretty sure he left out the part about me acting as an undercover bride."

"It's a good cover, Millie. Trust me on that. I've been doing this for a while. It's solid." Alex smiles at her uneasily. From the look on his face, I'm guessing he picked up on the edge in her voice, too. I'm not sure if that makes me feel better or worse.

"It might be a good plan if she left on her own. That remains to be seen," Millie says. "But if she was taken, me being there will be of absolutely no consequence to anyone. Unless you want to swap me for her."

Alex laughs until he sees the look on Millie's face. "No one is swapping anyone."

"Because after what I did to their network earlier this year," she continues, "I'm sure I'd be an attractive capture for them."

"Millie, we don't think the broader network even knows you were in on that takedown—even knows who you are. No one walked out of that house alive," Alex says. "You'll be fine. We're not going to let anything happen to you."

"No, we're not. We won't let anyone get near her," I say, quickly adding. "Or you."

Alex turns and looks at me. "Master Chief, you're not on this mission as our bodyguards. We'll be fine. We know how to protect ourselves. You're coming along to rescue Azayiz once we find her."

"We can do both," I say, locking my eyes with his.

"No, you really can't," he says as he starts to walk over to me. "We can't have you close to us in the hotel or you'll blow our cover."

"Our mission is always to protect our assets in a hostile country—in addition to whatever other elements are added," I say. "We're great multitaskers."

"The government of Pakistan provides protection for me, and we also have the hotel security. Your team will stay at the embassy until Azayiz's location is determined. Then we'll call you in," he says.

"My team," I say slowly, "is going to be in the hotel with you. My mission. My call. End of discussion."

He closes the distance between us, still smiling that bull-shit smile. "*Our* mission. Together. If you're in the hotel, you'll blow our cover. You will put us more at risk than if you stay at the embassy. It's only ten minutes away if we need you. Your job is to secure the HVT once identified, not to act as our cover."

Culver starts to say something, but stops when Millie says, "No, Alex. No. Part of the team is in the hotel with us. They're covert special operators. They know how to stay hidden. They won't blow anything. And I would feel better if they're ten seconds from us instead of ten minutes. They can be cover for us and still secure the target."

"Millie, you're more than capable of defending yourself and I will protect you if you need backup. This isn't your call," Alex says as he walks back toward her. I want to kill him so badly right now.

"It is my call," she says. "All of this is my call. If you want to use me as bait to catch my great-aunt, then we're going to do it how I want it done. If not, you can find someone else. I'll leave right now and fly back to San Diego. I've never wanted to be a part of this."

Alex looks from Millie to me. "One of them can stay in the hotel on a different floor."

"Same floor. Adjoining room. As many as they think is necessary. Their call. Not ours," Millie says.

He turns back around to look at her. "Millie."

Culver steps between them. "Agent Laskin, I know this is your first time working with us directly, so just to update you on protocol, we are solely responsible for how we man a mission. We appreciate your input, but we will decide how to proceed. I agree with Agent Marsh. We will have a few of our operators in an adjoining room. They'll stay out of your way unless you need them."

Alex takes a deep breath as he heads to the computer at the head table. He flips a few pictures up on the screen. "This is the last picture we have of Azayiz, and this man is her son, Fareed."

Millie lets out a soft gasp. All eyes turn to her. She looks at Alex. "So no one left the house alive, huh?"

"We were told no," Alex says slowly.

Millie walks up to the screen and points at Fareed's picture. "He drove the car the day I was kidnapped. He helped Yusef Hadzic take me," she says. "So that means they definitely know I was there that day. Everyone knows—so much for me not being a target."

Chapter Twenty-One

"Hey, asshole," Chase said, kicking Mack's hammock. "I asked you a question. Twice. You want to give me an answer? Or do I need to slap it out of you?"

Mack's mind snapped back into focus. "What was the question?"

"Man, what's wrong with you? You've been out of it all day," Chase said. "You better get it together before we land, or I'm pulling you from the mission."

"You thinking about that curvy, little brunette at the bar the other night?" Harry let out a long whistle. "Because I'm going to be honest, I've been thinking about her myself."

"Shut up, Culver." Mack reached over and gave the side of Harry's hammock a hard tug, almost sending him tumbling to the floor.

"What's the matter, man?" Harry said as he repositioned his body. "Don't tell me you couldn't close that deal."

"Yeah, like that's ever happened," Mack said. "But you're

welcome to call her now. The only thing you're ever going to get around me is sloppy seconds."

Chase laughed. "So what were you thinking about? I've never seen you that deep in thought. You trying out meditation or something?"

"Naw, I was thinking about Millie." Mack paused a second to control the shaking that was trying to come out in his voice. "If something ever happens to me, promise me that you have her—that you'll take care of her no matter what's happening in your lives."

Chase pulled himself up and looked over at Mack. "What are you talking about? You're two months away from retirement. You trying to jinx yourself? Keep that bullshit quiet."

Mack sunk down deeper into his hammock, so no one could see the tears that had started forming in his eyes. "Just promise me, man. I'm all she's got. If something happens, go get her away from my mom and take care of her. Please."

"Nothing's going to happen to you," Chase said. "But you already know we've got her if something does. Mar and I will adopt her. She'll be a part of our family. I will never let her out of my sight. I promise you that."

"I've got her, too," Harry said. "If anything happens to you, she's going to be smothered with attention from all her new uncles. She's going to be so sick of us, she'll probably try to hide."

Mack cracked a smile. "Actually, she probably will. She's developed a feisty, little independent streak. Don't let her push you away."

"When has anyone ever been able to resist me?" Harry

said. "Everyone loves me—mothers, daughters, babies, animals."

"Those goats in Ramadi really liked you a few months back," Clem chimed in from across the plane. "A little too much, for my liking."

Harry scooped up one of his boots from under his hammock and sent it flying across the plane—landing perfectly on Clem's stomach.

Mack turned to Chase and said quietly, "Just swear to me—"

"I've got you," Chase said. "Man, what's wrong with you? You're putting off some weird vibes. You starting to second-guess your retirement? Honestly, I am. I'm not sure if I'm ready to leave yet. The only thing that makes it right is that we're going out at the same time. And we're both moving to San Diego. You know?"

Mack took a deep breath. "Yeah. It's all going to be different now. But we have to do what's right for our families. Everything's about them. Have to keep them safe. Millie's the only reason I do anything. Since the day I first saw her in Sarajevo, everything's been for her. It's always going to be for her. Do you think she knows that?"

"What are you talking about?" Chase said. "That girl absolutely lives for you. She's devoted to you. You think she doesn't know you would walk through fire for her? Believe me, she knows."

"Yeah, I know she does," Mack said quietly.

"Whatever's bothering you, snap out of it. You're going to be with her in a few days," Chase said.

Mack looked across the plane and saw their CIA strap trying to discreetly signal him to the other side of the plane.

"I'm going to hit the head," Mack said to Chase as he walked away.

"It's going to happen tomorrow," George whispered as Mack got close to him. "You'll be clearing a little village outside of Fallujah. There's a house with a tunnel underneath. It has a red door, and it will have a black X on the side of it. Get in there alone. The tunnel's under the only table in the front room. We'll have agents in the tunnel. They'll blow the house when you're clear."

"How are we going to make sure no one else gets hurt in the blast?" Mack said.

"You need to be fast. See if you can bring up the rear of your clear line. We're going to have some distractions pulling the team forward and away from your house. They'll be fine. Our agents have radios. If anyone tries to follow you in, we'll call it off and try again later. You clear?"

Mack nodded his head. "Yeah. What happens after the house blows?"

"We'll get you to Baghdad, and then your buddy Azayiz is going to have some of her people meet us there. They'll help you get out of Iraq. I'm not sure how. Once we get you to Baghdad, we're done."

Mack nodded again. "Roger that."

"Good luck, Mack. I mean it," George said as he walked away.

Chapter Twenty-Two

MILLIE, VIRGINIA BEACH, VIRGINIA, 2020

Raine closes her office door behind me as I whip around to face her.

"What the fuck is going on?" I say as she cautiously walks by me to get behind her desk. "Did you know Mason and Alex were going to be here?"

"Mason got here yesterday. I only knew his team was going to be assigned to you this morning." She sits down in her chair and rolls it against the back wall, clearly trying to distance herself from the tirade that's about to come her way. "I figured he told you. Are you not together anymore?"

"We're not going to talk about my love life right now." I fling myself down in the chair across from her and scoot it back against the opposite wall.

"Oh, I think that's exactly what we're going to talk about. Your ex-boyfriend and your maybe-more-recently ex-boyfriend are both here preparing to go on a mission with you," she says, annoyingly not trying to suppress her laugh.

136

"This is like a really bad government version of *The Bachelorette*."

"That's not helpful, Raine," I say, shaking my head. "Did you know Alex was going to be here?"

"Absolutely not. That I definitely would have told you. How long has it been since you've seen him?"

"I haven't seen him since he took the assignment in Moscow. So what, like three or four years?"

"He's such an asshole, but he's still the prettiest man I've ever seen."

"Does he look good? Seriously, I didn't even look at him. I was so shocked. I think my eyes stopped working for a second."

The door opens slowly and I see Alex peeking his head through the crack like Jack Nicholson in *The Shining*. "Ladies, may I come in? Or is this a private conversation?" He comes in and closes the door without waiting for a reply.

"What are you doing here, Alex?" I say as he takes the chair next to me.

"What do you mean? I told you," he says as he pats my knee. "This is my assignment. I'm sorry George didn't tell you. I'm sure it was a shock to see me walk into that room."

"Why don't I let you two have a second to talk," Raine says, standing up.

"Wait, Raine. Stay for a second," Alex says. "I need to talk to both of you."

Raine stares at him coldly as she sits back down. She has never been a fan of his, and I've never understood why. She and I started at the agency together. We met Alex on our second day working at Langley. I thought he was charming. Raine thought he was full of shit.

Despite her ardent warnings, I started dating him a month after we met. We dated for almost a year until he got assigned to Moscow. He wanted me to move there with him—so much so that he proposed to me. I said no. He got pissed. After he got to Moscow, he called me nonstop for a month, trying to get me to change my mind. I finally had to tell him to quit calling. He got more pissed, but he stopped calling. I haven't heard from him since—until today.

"Millie, George told me you've tried to resign from the agency. I don't know what that's all about, but I know you're not particularly into this assignment. That was very apparent in the meeting."

"I'm fine. I've committed. I'll do my job."

"No, I know you will. You're good at your job, and I trust you. It's just that George told me you were in a relationship with the team leader, and that complicates things. His behavior —and yours, frankly—were inappropriate." I try to interrupt, but he holds up his hand. "No, let me finish. That wasn't a personal comment. You know as well as I do, it's a conflict of interest having him on this mission. I've tried to get another team without any luck, so it is what it is, but I need you and Raine to be on my side on this. On the agency's side. We need to keep this circle tight."

Before I can say anything, Raine jumps in. "This isn't high school, Alex. There are no sides. We're all on the same side. Master Chief Davis is the best operator in this entire building. I'm sure he'll be professional. We need to let him do his job."

"Raine," Alex says, his voice pouring out like silk, "I

know working in this building can start swaying your loyalties. These people are your co-workers now. But you work for the agency, and that's where your loyalty needs to be."

"I know where my loyalty needs to be. I'm loyal to the mission. And to complete this mission successfully, we all need to be on the same team. All of us—regardless of who signs our paychecks."

They're staring at each other so intensely that I wouldn't at all be shocked if fire started shooting out of their eyes. "Everyone needs to settle down," I say as I wave my hand to try to break their intense focus on each other. "Alex, you're in charge. Raine and I will follow your lead. Let's just get over there and get this done."

Raine shoots out of her chair. "Excuse me. I'll be right back."

Alex laughs as she slams the door. "So I guess she still doesn't like me, huh?"

"In her defense, you're kind of being an ass. What's all this Team Agency bullshit?"

He smiles. "I guess I'm feeling a little nostalgic for when we used to work together."

It's the first time I really look at his face. There are more wrinkles around his eyes than I remember, but the pale blue color still twinkles when he smiles. He has his beautiful, thick black hair slicked back away from his face—a few gray hairs around his temples. Raine was right about one thing: he is beautiful. That hasn't changed a bit.

"Millie," he says, reaching out to take my hand, "it's really good to see you again. You look absolutely gorgeous. You haven't changed at all."

I smile and squeeze his hand. "It's good to see you, too. You're as handsome as ever."

"I always did say we would make beautiful babies." He squeezes my hand softly before he lets it go. "Are you doing okay? With the kidnapping and everything . . . I wanted to call you after it all went down, but I wasn't sure if that would help or hurt."

"I'm fine. It was a lot, but it helped me answer some questions. It would have been nice if they could have been answered in a less traumatic fashion, but you know."

"I'm glad you found out about your mom. I know that's always nagged at you," he says, looking down at his feet. "That and your dad. It's coming up on nine years since he died. Has it gotten any easier?"

I'm assuming by the way he's talking he doesn't know about the agency helping my dad disappear—or at least claiming they did. I decide not to tell him.

"Yeah, it has," I say cautiously. "Mason's been really good at helping me mourn him."

He looks up. "Yeah. I mean, them doing the same job, I can understand that. So you're serious with this Mason guy or what?"

"Yeah. We've only been together for a few months, but we're serious."

"So no room for me to slip back in?" He smiles, his eyes twinkling like Christmas lights.

"Alex."

"I'm kidding, Millie," he says, laughing. "I know we're done. But maybe we can get back to being friends. I miss having you in my life. Seeing you has made that way more apparent."

"Maybe," I say as I smile back at him.

"Hey, I need to do a few things before we're wheels up," he says. "I'll see you on the plane. Save me a seat. I really want to catch up with you."

He pulls me up and hugs me. This time it doesn't feel shocking or weird. Honestly, it feels kind of nice—like coming home.

Chapter Twenty-Three

MASON, VIRGINIA BEACH, VIRGINIA, 2020

"Shut up, Mason. Shut up and let me finish," Raine says, quickly looking over her shoulder again.

"Shut up? Really? Someone's started feeling herself a little more in the few months I've been gone." I stop laughing when she grabs my shoulders and leans closer to my face. Raine is ultra-professional. There's absolutely no way she would ever touch me, especially not like this.

"I don't have much time. I think he's watching me. Shut up and let me finish," she says. "There's something off. I don't know what it is yet, but something's not right. The agent, Alex, they sent in for this—it's really suspicious. He and Millie have a history. It's a weird choice for this assignment. I don't trust him at all."

"What do you mean they 'have a history'?"

"She met him when we were first at the agency. They dated for about a year." She pauses for a second. "She really needs to tell you the rest."

"Raine, just tell me."

She shakes her head and sighs. "Fine. When he got transferred to Moscow, he asked her to go with him." She looks away from me. "He proposed to her. She said no. It got sticky."

"Sticky how?"

"He was pissed. He stalked her for a while. More than normal breakup stuff. He was obsessed."

"So you think she feels uncomfortable having him around? It's only for a few days." I'm trying to process why Millie would date such a douche, but I'm not understanding the urgency in Raine's voice. "I'll take care of her. I won't let him do anything to her."

"No, it's more than that," she says, starting to pace. "He gave us a pep talk about how we needed to be loyal to the agency—at the expense of our partnership with the teams. It was a real "them or us" kind of vibe. It's off. I can't explain."

"Does he know Millie and I are together? Maybe he's just marking his territory. It's a guy thing. It's no big deal," I say, shrugging.

"Mason, what have you said about my intuition?"

"That it's freaky."

"That it's freaky accurate. Trust my intuition on this. Something's off."

I take a deep breath. "Did she tell you about her dad?"

"What about her dad?" She scrunches up her face and grabs the side of my locker wall like she's bracing for a hurricane-force wind.

"That George guy she works for told her he might still be alive."

"Excuse me? What the fuck!" she says, slamming her hand against the wall. "I wondered why she changed her mind about coming back. George is an asshole. He will play any card to win."

"That's what Chase and I told her."

"Chase? You mean her dad's friend?" She stops herself from saying more.

"Yeah. Why? Does that mean something to you?"

"No. It's just . . . you know, I met him when they got back from Bosnia."

She's not nearly as good a liar as Millie is. "Raine, what are you holding back?"

She looks at me blankly. "I don't know enough to tell you. Really. I'm supposed to be briefed on something this afternoon that apparently involves Chase."

"Huh," I say, stroking my beard. "I can't imagine what Chase's involvement would be in this. He's been retired for a while now. Did you know George was the spook assigned to his team—to Millie's dad's team?"

"What? No. George didn't know Millie's dad."

I nod my head slowly. "He did. He had your job here when Millie's dad was on the teams. He knew him well."

"Wow," she says, leaning against the wall. "This is even weirder than I thought."

"Yeah. Millie—" I'm cut off by the sound of someone punching the security code into the door. Raine dives behind the back of the lockers as the door opens. It's Alex.

"What are you doing in here?" I stand up to block his view of where Raine is now hiding.

"Hey. I'm looking for Raine. Have you seen her?" He

smiles broadly like he's trying to hypnotize me with alarmingly white teeth.

"Naw, man. I haven't seen her. She doesn't really hang out in here. Really an operator-only area." I'm trying to keep my tone somewhat civil.

"Ah, yeah. Well someone saw her come in here a few minutes ago." He's still smiling. I'm wondering how many people have fallen for his bullshit charm and why Millie was one of them.

"You're welcome to look around," I say, mocking him as I gesture around the small room. "Maybe she's hiding in Hawk's locker."

He glances over at Hawk, who is lounging back in his chair. Hawk spreads his legs a little wider as he hugs his rifle lovingly to his chest. "Knock yourself out, man," Hawk says, nodding toward the small opening he's left to walk into his locker. Alex ignores his challenge. I guess he's a little smarter than he looks.

Bryce comes around the corner pushing the laundry cart—full of towels and T-shirts that were just washed yesterday. And I'm guessing Raine's underneath there somewhere.

Alex eyes Bryce suspiciously. "A couple hours until wheels up and you're doing laundry? Kind of late for that, don't you think?"

"You know what they say about idle hands," Bryce says as he tries to walk around Alex. Alex stops the cart with his foot and looks directly at me.

I smile. "You know, Bryce, laundry is a rookie job. Alex is more of a rookie here than you are. Maybe he'll do the laundry for you today."

"I don't think we're in need of anyone doing laundry right now," Alex says, looking down at the basket.

"Friend, that depends entirely on how you want us to smell for the next ten hours on the plane." Butch puts his arm around Alex and looks at him with his best I-dare-you-to-challenge-me smile.

JJ takes his shirt off as he walks over to stand on the other side of Alex. He tosses the shirt in the laundry basket. "My shirt needs to be washed while you're at it, Alex."

Alex's smile slowly fades away as he looks up at JJ flexing his massive pecs. "Naw, bruh. I'm going to pass. You'll let Raine know I'm looking for her if you see her?"

"Sure," JJ says. "Bruh."

Alex turns around slowly and lets himself out. As the door clicks shut, I reach into the basket and lift Raine out. "Bryce, you're never in charge of strategy. Worst plan ever," I say, shaking my head. "Go put this laundry in again in case he's watching."

Hawk pulls Raine behind the door as Bryce wheels the laundry cart out. "I'll take her out in my duffel bag," Hawk says as he pulls her into his locker.

"What? I'm not going to fit in your duffel." Raine tries and fails to walk around Hawk.

"You're barely over five feet. I've fit grown men in here," Hawk says as he picks her up and starts stuffing her body into the bag.

"In fairness, the men were dead, though," Butch says as he watches Raine protest fruitlessly. "Dead bodies are usually more malleable, you know?"

Just before Hawk pulls the duffel string closed over her

face, I say, "Wait until our plane takes off, and then call Chase. I'll text you his number."

From somewhere inside the bag, she says, "Don't text me. They might be monitoring my phone. I hope I'm being paranoid, but we can't take any chances. You think there's any way Culver is in on whatever this might be?"

"Not a chance in hell. He has Chase's number. Get him involved. And let me know what you find out in your briefing."

Hawk easily slings her over his shoulder and starts out the door.

I grab Butch by the shoulder and push him after them. "Go with him. After you dump her somewhere, gently extract Millie from wherever she is and bring her in here. Make sure Alex doesn't see."

"Roger that," Butch says as the door closes behind him.

Chapter Twenty-Four

I've only had a second alone with Raine since the meeting. I'm sensing she wants to discuss something privately with me, and we still haven't talked about her going to Iraq with Chase. I need to get her by herself, but Alex won't leave us alone. She left her office about a half hour ago. Alex followed her, but he's back now without her. I've texted her a couple times, but no response.

"I'll be right back," I say to Alex.

Alex stands up. "Where are you going?" he says quickly, and then tries to act casually uninterested. Something's off with him. I can't quite place it.

"The bathroom," I say as I brush by him. "Would you like to come with me?"

"Yes. I would actually like to go everywhere with you." His megawatt smile accentuates the sugary-smooth tone of his voice.

I roll my eyes as I walk out the door. "The charm doesn't work on me anymore, Alex."

"I don't believe that for a second." I hear him laughing as I close the door.

I take the long way to the bathroom, so I can look in the situation room for Raine. It's empty. As I turn around, I see the top of Alex's head moving around the corner just a tad too late. Since he seems to be watching me, I head to the bathroom. I'm sitting in the stall, trying to figure out what's happening when I see feet wearing male boots walking in. Alex is apparently done hiding from me. I open the door, ready to confront him, and jump back when I see Hawk and Butch standing there.

"What are you guys doing in here?" I look quickly from them to the empty duffel bag Hawk is now holding up. He grins from ear to ear, looking like a ten-year-old holding up a fish he just caught.

"Okay," I say as I back up into the stall. "I'm not sure what's going on here, but y'all need to get out of my way, so I can leave."

"Sorry, Mills. No can do," Butch says as he covers the ground between us and picks me up like a baby in one fluid motion. Hawk holds the bag as Butch starts to feed my feet through the opening.

I jerk my feet away from the bag. "What the fuck? Butch! Put me down!"

Butch ignores me and looks up at Hawk. "I hate it when they struggle."

"Yeah. It takes so much more time," Hawk says as he

grabs both my feet with one of his massive hands. He pulls down hard on my legs as he shoves my feet into the bag.

"Ow!" I say, backhanding him hard on the cheek. He doesn't react.

"Mason said to extract her 'gently,'" Butch says as he lifts my upper body higher, so Hawk can keep force-funneling my legs into the bag.

"How does gently work again?" Hawk looks thoughtfully at Butch as he pulls the bag over my waist.

"Man, I've never really been sure. Maybe they should teach a BUD/S course on that."

In a matter of seconds, I'm standing between them with the duffel bag up to my chest. I desperately grab the top of the bag before they can pull it all the way over my head.

"Mills, do you want to get the rest of the way into the bag by yourself or do you need my help?" Hawk says, smiling mischievously at me as he gently taps his fingers on my hands.

"Will you at least tell me where you're taking me?" I try to discreetly push the bag down a little bit. Butch pulls it back up from behind me.

"I guess we could tell her," Hawk says, looking over me to Butch.

"Man, I don't feel much like talking right now to be honest." Butch pulls the bag a little higher.

"Look at that, Mills. Even Butch doesn't have anything to say. Guess it's time for you to be quiet, too." Hawk flips my clenched fingers off the bag and holds my hands gently, giving me one last chance to comply on my own.

"I hate you both so much right now," I say with all the

drama I can muster as I put my arms in the bag and start to sink down.

"That's rude," Hawk says as he pulls the duffel string closed over my head.

"And hurtful," Butch adds.

"And hurtful," Hawk repeats, emphasizing each word with light taps to my now fully covered head. Hawk picks me up and slings me over his shoulder. I try unsuccessfully to conform naturally to his body.

"You weigh a lot more than Raine," he says.

"Um, first of all, fuck you," I say from within the bag. "And second, have you been walking around the building stuffing women into bags all day?"

"Mind your own business, Millie," Butch says.

"Butch," Hawk says as he starts walking, "Millie said she hated me. That hurts my feelings."

"I know, big guy," Butch says, flicking my shoulder through the bag. "But she's just projecting her anger at Mason on to you. She didn't mean it."

"I kept her from getting shot a few months ago. You think at least I could get some gratitude." Hawk grabs my face through the bag and shaking it playfully.

"Stop it!" I say, laughing as I unsuccessfully try to hit Hawk.

"People in bags don't get to talk, Millie," Hawk says.

"Again, they're usually dead though," Butch says.

"True. True. A lot easier that way, to be honest," Hawk says as he stops walking.

I can't see anything through the bag, but I hear what I

think is a code being punched into a door. We take a few steps forward, and a door slams behind us.

"Good God, please tell me Millie's not in that bag." I hear Mason's voice as Hawk places me on the floor and unties the drawstring to let me out. I stand up and see I'm in the operators' ready room. Mason's entire team is there doing last checks on their gear before we go wheels up. They're all looking at us and laughing except Mason, who's shaking his head in disbelief. He looks at Hawk. "Man, what part of *gently* don't you understand?"

"As it turns out, pretty much all of it," Hawk says as he lifts me out of the bag.

"I think you should probably leave before Millie beats the crap out of you." Mason looks from me to Hawk.

"Nope. Not until she apologizes." Hawk folds his arms as he looks at me, his eyes twinkling.

"You shoved me into a duffel bag and you want *me* to apologize?" I say, shaking my head at him.

"You said you hated me. That's way worse." Hawk's scowl is starting to break as he hears the laughing around him.

"Would it make you feel better if I told you I hate all of them, too?" I sweep my hands around the room.

"Somewhat better. At least I wouldn't feel like I'm being singled out." Hawk finally starts laughing. He throws his head back in disgust—mad that he couldn't keep a straight face a little longer. He steps forward and hugs me. "Hey, Mills. I'm glad you're back. We've missed you."

Pretty soon the entire team—except JJ—is around me in a big, suffocating group hug. That lasts a few seconds when I hear Mason from across the room. "All right. All right. That's plenty."

After I'm released from the scrum, I walk over to Mason's locker. "What the hell?"

"Sorry about that. I asked them to bring you to me. I had no idea they were going to do that."

"You asked them to bring me to you? What, are you like the king now?"

"Millie, do you want to fight right now?"

"No," I say, sighing. "I really don't."

"Look. Raine said Alex might be watching you guys. I don't know if she's just being paranoid or not, but I wanted to make sure he didn't see you come in here."

"He's not watching me—in the way she means it, anyway."

"So in what way is he watching you?" Mason's eyes lock into mine as I shift uncomfortably. "Tell me what I need to know here, Mills."

"What you need to know professionally or personally?"

"Sounds like we're going to need to cover both."

I try to lean casually against his locker, but I know my folded arms give away my extreme discomfort with this subject. "We met at the agency. We dated. He got transferred to Moscow. He asked me to come along. I said no."

He nods his head—his lips pursed—like he's trying to make sure what he says next comes out right. "And he asked you to marry him?"

"Does Raine tell you everything?" I rub my temples to try to stop the headache that's forming.

"Well you clearly don't. Why have you never told me about him?"

I shrug. "I haven't talked to him in like four years. There's not much to tell. Have you told me about all your exes?"

"I've told you about all my exes who are going to be on this mission with us."

"Cute," I say. "And I had no idea he was going to be here today."

"Raine said he tried to pit the agency against the teams. What's that about?"

"I don't know. I think she's exaggerating that a little bit. He's just new to management. He's been a lone wolf in the field so long. I think he's just trying to shore up his team."

"Interesting technique."

"He's not like you guys. He's used to being on his own. You know the whole 'working in the shadows' thing. He's good at his job."

"So you trust him?"

"I mean sure. As much as I trust anyone at the agency."

"That's not a ringing endorsement."

"Look, I'm sorry I asked for your team to be pulled."

He smiles very slightly like he does when he knows I'm not telling him the truth. "Don't apologize for something you would do again in a second."

He's not wrong, and he knows it. We stand there for a minute, staring at each other silently.

"Are we good?" I say. "I have a few things I need to do before we leave."

"We're good. I told you before I'll always have your back whether or not we're together."

My heart drops all the way to my toes. "What does that mean? Are we not together anymore?"

"I don't know, Millie. You really pissed me off by trying to call my team off the mission. And I know you're hiding stuff from me again. Let's just get this over with, and then we can talk about it," he says, looking away from me. "But for purposes of this mission, we're definitely not together."

I shake my head to try to register what he's saying. "Wow. Okay." I take a step back. He's still not looking at me. "Am I allowed to leave on my own? Or do you want to have your guys stuff me in a bag again?"

He motions his arm toward the door. "Knock yourself out."

I swing the door open with so much force, I'm actually surprised when it doesn't come off its hinges. I turn around, hoping he's looking at me. He's not.

Chapter Twenty-Five

I'm already on the plane when Millie walks in. She's with Alex. He says something that makes her smile. She pushes him playfully on the shoulder. He laughs. They head over to the bench on the far side of the plane—away from us. I'm not exactly sure how I'm feeling, but none of it's good.

I watch them buckle in. It takes me back to carrying Millie onto the plane after she fainted coming back from our last mission together. She was in shock from having just survived her first firefight. I remember strapping her limp body in and holding her while the plane took off.

"You going to be able to stay objective about this mission?" JJ's voice snaps me out of my trance.

I turn away from Millie and walk back over to our side of the plane. "It's not going to be a problem."

"You sure about that?" JJ says as he sits down beside me. "I don't know what it is about her, but you lose focus when she's around."

I turn and scowl at him. "I'm fine."

"Seriously, though. What is it about her? I've seen you cycle through your share of women. None of them have made you like this. She's hot, no denying that, but there are a lot of hot women out there who are a lot less high maintenance."

"She's not high maintenance."

"Bruhhhhh," he says. "C'mon now."

I laugh. "Yeah. Okay. She's a little high maintenance. But she's also smart and funny. Sassy. And God, she's so sweet."

"Sweet?" he says, laughing. "Since when do you like sweet?"

"Since I met her."

"So all it takes is some girl being nice to you for you to throw away your career. Man, your childhood must have been more fucked up than I know."

"It's not like that."

"So what's it like? You love your new job? You like giving up your team to teach a bunch of dumbass recruits?"

"No, man. I don't," I say, sighing. "I miss this every day."

"I'm glad you're back. This is your team. This is where you belong." He pauses and then adds, "When Stevie's healed up, he can take another team. You need to stay here. You want that, right?"

"Do I want to lead this team again? Yeah. But it's more complicated than that now."

"Because of her?" he says, shaking his head. "I don't get it. Look at her over there. She's flirting with her old boyfriend —a guy that she almost married. That's okay with you?"

"She didn't almost marry him."

"You know that? She told you that?"

"She actually didn't tell me anything. This is the first I'm hearing about him."

"Oh, so she's keeping stuff from you again? Like all that shit about her family. The last time we worked with her, she kind of forgot to mention the man we were going after was her uncle. Uncle Sayid—one of the most-wanted terrorists in the world. Might have been nice if we knew that."

"Man, what's your problem?" I say, turning to look at him. "You've never liked her—personally or professionally."

"My problem isn't with her professionally. She's fine. Spooks are always giving us half the story. That's more of the same. My problem is that she changes you. You lose perspective and focus. You become somebody else. You're in too deep to see it."

I stare at him for a good minute. I'm pissed at Millie right now, but that doesn't give anyone else the right to come at her. "Look, man. You're my best friend. That's never going to change. But you're wrong about this. Let's just focus on the mission."

"All right," he says, standing up. "Just promise me you're going to be one hundred percent objective."

I nod. "One hundred percent."

After he walks away, I look back over to where Millie and Alex were sitting. He's still there. She's not. I stand up to look around the plane. I don't see her up in the work area. I take a stroll around and finally see her lying on a bench tucked away under the storage cabinets. She's curled up in a little ball with her jacket pulled over her head. She looks like she's freezing, which I know from experience she probably is.

Unfortunately, I don't have the five blankets she usually

requires to get warm. Luckily, our logistics team packed our parkas. I told them we wouldn't need them in the spring in Pakistan, but they like to cover all their bases. I grab my coat and walk over to her. I watch her sleep for a second. She looks so sweet and vulnerable. I want to spoon up behind her and keep her warm. I gently cover her with my coat and take off my fleece and put it under her head. She doesn't stir. I still don't understand how someone can sleep that deeply.

As I turn around, I see Alex walking over to me.

"Master Chief. May I have a word with you?" He's nodding over to an area away from Millie. I motion him to go first.

"What's up?" I say as we get over to the private area.

"Bluntly, I know you have feelings for Agent Marsh." He's looking directly in my eyes, challenging me. I just stare at him. "I understand that. Believe me. More than you know. But as soon as we land, she needs to be all-in as my wife. She needs to play the role to perfection if we want to have a successful mission. Having you around—staring at her—is not going to help anything. Maybe you should stay at the embassy and assign a few of your team members to the hotel."

I smile. "How about you do your job and I'll do mine?"

He takes a step closer to me. I know he's trying to provoke me. If I take a swing at him, I'm off the mission.

"I need for you to stay away from Millie after we land," he says, leaning in—just inches from my face.

My hands automatically clench into fists. "And I need for you to back the fuck off me," I whisper.

JJ appears out of nowhere and wedges himself between us, facing Alex. He starts pushing me backward with his body.

"Agent Laskin," he says, "thank you for your input. We'll take your suggestions into consideration."

Alex smiles and nods his head slowly as he walks away. JJ turns to me and keeps pushing me back. "How's that objectivity working for you, Mase?"

Chapter Twenty-Six

As the helicopter landed just outside the village, Mack made sure he was the last one off. He took the rear position in the line as they started their approach. They covered the quarter mile quickly. It didn't seem like anyone was around. George told the team this morning that locals reported an Al Qaeda leader hiding out there. When they got within a couple hundred yards, Mack saw the small house with the red door and the black X. Most of the houses had some kind of color on them, so it didn't stand out too much, but Mack thought they could have been a little more subtle.

When the rest of the team had passed the house, he heard voices coming from a house about a hundred feet in front of their position. The rest of the team started hustling that way. Mack swerved to the right and entered through the red door. He saw the table. He pushed it aside and opened the trap door.

As he climbed down into the dimly lit tunnel, he heard the house explode above him. He instinctively flung his body to the ground and covered his head. The tunnel walls shook violently, but didn't collapse. He quickly got to his feet and flipped his goggles down to help see through the wall of dust ahead of him. He saw two people in front of him—motioning for him to follow. He heard his team in the distance scream his name. As the tunnel began to clear, he started running. It only took a few minutes for their screaming voices to fade out behind him.

"Mack!" Chase screamed. "Mack! Answer me!"

"Mack!" The entire team screamed his name as they tried to get close enough to the burning rubble to look for his body that they knew wasn't there. The building had been blown into small bits, and they knew anyone inside it had suffered the same fate. Still, they screamed his name—hoping for a miracle.

Suddenly gunfire began to rain down on them from the hills above the village. As they began taking fire, they all jumped behind whatever cover they could find.

"Where's it coming from?" Clem yelled as a round split the rock above his head. He scrunched down farther and poked his rifle out. A bullet hit the dirt in front of him. He rolled back behind the rock.

Chase made it behind a building. He peered around the side through his rifle scope. "We've got at least ten on that southeastern ridge. They've got good cover," he shouted above the gunfire.

The rest of his team was spread out within twenty feet of

him. They were all trying to return fire, but Chase knew they didn't have position. They were basically sitting ducks. He didn't quite understand why the enemy were only firing from one position. If they spread out at all, they could have made quick work of his team.

"Alpha One to Base," Chase said, lowering his microphone into position.

"This is Base. You got a sit rep for me?"

"Nothing good. We have one down. House exploded around him. He's gone. We're taking fire from the southeast. What do you see on the satellite?"

"Southeast looks like about twenty tangoes. I'm not seeing any more surrounding. You've got an easy escape path at the north-northwest position. I have a bird incoming. Five mikes out. Can you hold until then?"

"Yeah. We've got it."

Chase looked over to the exploded building. He was half hoping to see Mack walk over, like a phoenix rising from the ashes. All he saw was burning embers of nothing. He fought back the tears coming to his eyes, leveled his rifle, and started returning fire.

Chapter Twenty-Seven

MILLIE, IN-FLIGHT, VIRGINIA BEACH TO ISLAMABAD, 2020

I wake up with Mason's scent in my nose. I had a dream about him, so I think it's probably just in my mind until I realize someone covered me with a coat and put something under my head. I lift my head up slightly to see the gray fleece he was wearing earlier now folded up like a pillow. I look around to see if anyone's watching before I bury my head in it and take a deep breath. That's definitely where the scent's coming from. It smells like him—musky, sweaty, and a little bit like vanilla. I take another breath. I want to go back to sleep with my face buried in it.

"So are you finally awake?" Unfortunately, it's not Mason's voice.

I look up to see Alex standing above me. I sit up quickly and shake my head to get my focus back. "Yeah. How long have I been asleep?"

"Like five hours. I've never seen you sleep like that. You used to be such a light sleeper when we were together."

"Are we almost there?"

"A few more hours," he says, pulling the coat off me. He holds his hand out to help me stand up. "You should probably get dressed pretty soon."

I look down at myself. "I am dressed."

"I mean dressed like a bride on her honeymoon and less like a CIA agent," he says, leading me to the restrooms. I pull my hand away from his. "When we land, I'm going to be holding your hand, kissing you—doing what newlyweds do. You need to start getting into your role."

"We haven't landed yet." I narrow my eyes. I'm just starting to realize what's going to happen over the next few days. It's unsettling. I try to brush it off. "I brought a few changes of clothes, but they're all pretty much like this," I say, gesturing at my outfit.

"Yeah, I figured." He holds up a garment bag. "The agency bought you some vacation-like clothes. I knew you wouldn't have time to think about that."

I stare at him for a second. "Do you really think this is necessary?"

"Yeah, I do. You need to trust me. You've never been in the field like this. You need to completely transform yourself into my wife in the next hour or so. There's a shalwar kameez in there and head scarves. There's some Western clothes, too. Hope they fit you. I was going off memory." He smiles at me. "I'll give you some privacy so you can change."

When he walks out of sight, I unzip the bag. It's full of beautiful, colorful clothes. I don't want any of them. I'm starting to think George was right when he told me my disposition was much too overt to ever work in the field. Unfortunately, I don't have much choice in the matter right now.

I dig through the bag and choose a light green, silk sweater and black slacks. They fit perfectly. I find black pumps with a heel higher than I've ever worn in my life. I slip them on and wrap a multicolored, fringy scarf around my neck. I splash some water on my face and put my hair back in a conservative knot. There are no mirrors on the plane, so I'm just going to have to guess I look the part.

I walk around the corner and run smack into Mason. He almost knocks me off my four-inch heels. He grabs my shoulders to steady me.

"Wow," he says, pushing me back a little to look at me. "This is a new look for you."

"I'm supposed to look like a wife. I don't even know what that means," I say, shaking my head. "Do I look completely idiotic?"

"No," he says, giving my body a quick scan. "Not at all. You look beautiful. And tall. Why are you so tall?"

I lift my foot as he looks down. "I'm going to last about an hour in these."

"I'm going to place money on less than that," he says, laughing. "Hey, come over here for a second."

He nods toward a bench.

"What's up?" I say, sitting down next to him.

"I want to apologize for snapping at you earlier. I was mad you tried to call my team off the mission, but I didn't mean any of that other stuff. Of course we're still together. You know that, right?"

"I think I do," I say slowly. "I hope I do."

"This is harder than I thought. I've never had a problem separating personal from professional—partially because I didn't have much of a personal life before. But now, with the way I feel about you, it's almost impossible. This is new for me."

"It's new for me, too. I asked for another team because I knew I couldn't focus as well if you were on the mission."

"Yeah. Now that we're here, I understand that. But we have to separate it or we're going to make mistakes. For purposes of this mission, you have to be any other agent, and I have to be any other operator."

I take a deep breath. "I completely agree. It's the only way we can do this."

"Look, Millie, I know you're holding back information from me again." He locks his eyes with mine. "It's a problem."

"Yeah. There's some stuff the agency director told me that he asked me not to share—with anyone."

"Here's how it is for me: I tell you everything. And if you think there's something I'm leaving out, ask me and I will tell you the entire truth. I know trust is an issue for you. I know you're working on it, but if we're going to make it, you can't hide stuff from me. Do you get that?"

"Yeah," I say, looking down.

"That's all I'm going to say about it now. Think about it," he says, tilting my chin up. "I can't be in this relationship with only half of you."

"I understand."

"One more thing. Are you into Alex? At all? Is there any part of you that wants to be back with him?"

"Zero. Absolutely no interest in being back with him."

He smiles and nods. "We're getting ready to land. Mission-mode activated. Agent Marsh, are you ready for this assignment? Is there anything I can do to help you?"

"Thank you for asking, Master Chief. I'm actually a little nervous. I'm not sure how good I'm going to be at acting like someone else."

"You'll be fine. You're the smartest person I know. Focus on one thing at a time—slow and steady."

I nod and look up at him. "Hey, by the way, thanks for covering me up. And the pillow. I was cold."

"I figured," he says, quickly squeezing my hand.

"Can I keep the fleece in case the hotel room is cold?"

"I don't why it should be different than every other sweatshirt I own." He smiles as he stands up. He pats my shoulder. "You're the best at this, Agent Marsh. You're going to be fine."

As he walks away, I close my eyes and give myself an internal pep talk. When I'm satisfied that my mind's straight, I walk over and sit next to my "husband."

"Hey," Alex says. "You look great. Didn't want to try the shalwar, huh?"

"Maybe later. It's really pretty."

He reaches out and holds my hand. I take a deep breath and begrudgingly let him.

"What's your name?"

"Millie Laskin."

He smiles at me. "How long have we been married?"

"Two weeks. We got married on April 11 in a small, private wedding."

"Too much detail," he says. "Keep your answers as short as possible. Islamabad is a progressive city, but they're still not used to women being chatty. That actually helps you—less to think about."

"Surprisingly, I like thinking."

He rolls his eyes. "Remember, you're an actor playing a role. No one's asking you to become this person for the rest of your life. Just a few days. A week, tops."

I nod. "I guess we're staying in the same room. Are there two beds?"

"We're staying in the honeymoon suite. There's one bed."

"So you'll be sleeping on the floor then or maybe they have a couch?"

"Millie," he says as he puts his hand on my leg, "this is a hotel. There are people everywhere—maids and food service in our room. We have a 24-hour butler. We have to be on all the time."

"I'm guessing actual consummation of the marriage can be off the table. Or are you expecting to get laid?"

"Ah, there's the sarcasm," he says, rolling his eyes again. "You know, it's one of my least favorite things about you."

"Funny because it's one of my favorite things about me."

As the pilot announces the landing, he takes his hand off my leg and sighs. I lean back and close my eyes. I've never dreaded anything in my life as much as I'm dreading these next few days. And that includes my dad's funeral. At least I was still in shock for that.

Chapter Twenty-Eight

MASON, ISLAMABAD, PAKISTAN, 2020

"Mrs. Laskin, it's a pleasure to finally meet you. Your husband has said such lovely things about you." A man bows slightly as Millie and Alex walk hand-in-hand out of the plane. What looks like a delegation from the Pakistan government gestures them toward a waiting limousine.

"It's my pleasure," Millie says. "I've been so looking forward to spending time in your beautiful country."

She's pulled the scarf up to cover her head. I can't see her face, but her words sound sincere. She might be better at this than she thought.

"You okay?" Ty walks up behind me.

"Yeah, I'm all good. Let's get geared up. You're driving. Stay on them, but we need to arrive a few minutes after them."

He nods as he walks down toward our waiting SUV. I've already sent JJ, Hawk, and Mouse to the embassy with our extra supplies—rifles, ammo, body armor, night vision. The government agreed to let some of us stay in the hotel, but we're only allowed one pistol and three extra mags each. I've never been this lightly armed on a mission. I don't like it at all. When Millie's head disappears into the limousine, I climb into the SUV.

"I wish one of us could be in there with her," I mutter under my breath.

"She'll be fine," Butch says. "If anything happens, we're on her in no more than ten seconds."

I nod. I've prepared for everything I think can go wrong on this mission, but I know there's still so many variables I haven't accounted for—and that's making me more tense than usual.

"Bryce, you manage to get those extra mags out of the plane?" I ask.

"Yeah. They're in my shorts. If they search for them, I'm at least hoping the pat-down will be by a woman."

"Good luck with that in Pakistan," Butch says. "And you're using those mags. I don't want to even touch them."

Ty pulls into the outer circle of the reception area at the hotel. We watch as Millie and Alex exit the limousine—still annoyingly holding hands. When they disappear into the hotel, we pull up to the valet.

"Welcome, gentlemen," the valet says. "If you'll step out, I'll have someone park your car."

"Thanks, chief, but I'm going to park my own car. Just point me in the right direction," Ty says.

The valet starts to protest when a man walks quickly up to him. "Let them park their own car. Americans have different needs than we do."

He turns to me. "Welcome to the Serena. I'm the hotel

manager. The Ministry Secretary has told me privately you are part of Mr. Laskin's delegation," he says quietly. "I arranged for you to stay in an adjoining room to their suite. Of course, the door can be locked from either side . . . if the newlyweds require privacy."

"Good to know," I say, grabbing my key cards out of his hand.

"Room 402," he says, looking down. "And I'm assuming you have adhered to the government's rules on weaponry."

"You're welcome to check our bags if you like." I motion toward where Butch and Bryce are standing. Bryce waves his arm over our luggage as he peers at the manager over the top of his sunglasses.

"That won't be necessary," the manager says as he walks away as quickly as he came.

When we get in the room, I try to open the adjoining door. It's still locked on their side. I knock. Millie opens it almost immediately. She's holding a change of clothes including undergarments. I hope she knows she's not changing in front of him.

"Master Chief," Alex says as he marches over to me. "As I've already told you, we have eyes watching us at all times. We're supposed to be strangers. We can't have you coming into our room."

I ignore him and look back at Millie. "You okay?"

She smiles and nods. "I'm good. We're getting ready to have dinner on the patio off the lobby. And hopefully start making contacts with some of Azayiz's old friends."

"You want to change in our room? I'll make the guys leave."

"It's not like I haven't seen her naked before," Alex says, laughing.

"Alex!" Millie jumps between us. "Completely inappropriate."

"Oh, I'm inappropriate, but he's not?" He gestures toward me. Millie has her back pressed firmly against me—trying to hold me back. I'm not moving. He's still trying to provoke me. It's not going to work.

"That statement was inappropriate, Alex. Get yourself under control." Millie looks up at me. "I'm changing in the bathroom. He will, too. No one is seeing anyone else naked."

She disappears into the bathroom. I hear the door lock.

"We're getting ready to leave for dinner," Alex says, motioning me to the door.

"Great. I could use a bite to eat." I hold up my hand to stop him from replying. "We're not going to eat with you, but we are going to be there—within ten to twenty feet of you."

"I don't think that's the best idea," he says.

"Thanks for your input," I say, turning around to go back in my room. "Bryce, you want to have dinner? Alex is buying."

"Hell yes. I'm starving."

I turn around as I start to close the adjoining door. "This door stays unlocked. If I try it and it's locked, I will break it down. You understand?"

He glares at me. I close the door behind me and stand there, waiting to hear the sound of the door locking. He's stupid enough to try it. I don't hear it. He must be learning. I look at Ty and Butch. "After we leave, sweep both rooms for bugs and cameras. Look into Agent Laskin's gear. Let me know what weapons he's carrying. And jam some wire into that dead bolt to make sure he can't lock it."

"Roger that," Butch says.

Millie's sitting alone at the table when we walk into the courtyard. She's wearing a dark blue dress with what looks like glittery diamonds all over it. Her hair is flowing down her back and shining even brighter than the dress. If she wants people to notice her, mission accomplished. Every eye in the room is on her.

Alex is nowhere to be seen. I'm instantly pissed off. So much for him having her back. I ask the host to seat us at a table separated from her table only by a row of thick palm plants. Millie sees us walk to our table.

As we sit down, the waiter approaches her table and bows slightly. "Mrs. Laskin, welcome to the Serena. Is this your first time in Pakistan?"

"It is," Millie says. "I hope to get out and explore. I've heard Islamabad is a beautiful city. My great-aunt was born in Pakistan."

"Really? You have Pakistani blood?"

"No. She married my great-uncle—a Bosnian. One side of my family is Bosnian. The other is American."

"Interesting. Does your aunt live in Pakistan now?"

"I really don't know. I've lost touch with that side of my family. Her name is Azayiz Custovic. I'm not sure of her given last name—her Pakistani name. Custovic is her married name."

Even with my obstructed view through the palms, I can clearly see the waiter should never play poker. Millie has to be catching the shock on his face. Alex walks up from behind the waiter and sits down. The waiter jumps slightly.

"I think my wife has enough water," Alex says, gesturing to the water pitcher in the waiter's hand.

"Yes, sir. Of course. Enjoy your meal."

"What was that about?" Alex says as he watches the waiter walk away.

"Oh, just small talk about the city. I dropped Azayiz's name. He didn't bite," she says.

Although her tone is smooth, I know she's lying to him. I've seen her pick up almost undetectable facial tics when she's interrogating someone. There's no way she missed the waiter's face when she said Azayiz's name.

"Surely we'll find someone at the hotel who knows her. Give it time. Let's just enjoy our dinner. Have some wine. Talk about old times," he says, reaching across the table to stroke her arm. "And maybe some new times . . ."

She pulls her arm back. "Alex, this is just an assignment. Purely professional. I know we both have roles to play, but let's not get them confused with reality."

He says something quietly to her that I can't hear. She smiles at him, but I can tell she's uncomfortable. I want to pull her away from him so badly.

"You want to switch seats so you don't have such a good view?" Bryce says.

"I'm good," I say, not taking my eyes off Alex. I tune back into their conversation.

"Hey," Alex says as he pours Millie a glass of wine. "I haven't seen Mason down here. Maybe he's finally starting to realize you can take care of yourself."

175

"Yeah, maybe. He's really not that persistent," she says. "Or protective, for that matter."

I smile. The sarcasm is definitely meant for me. She knows it's one of my favorite things about her.

Chapter Twenty-Nine

VIRGINIA BEACH, VIRGINIA, AUGUST 6, 2011

Chase knocked on Millie's door gently. She had been staying in their guest room since Mack died. Mack asked him to get Millie away from his mom if anything happened to him. That's what Chase did. He delivered the news about Mack's death to Camille and Millie, and told Camille he was taking Millie. Camille put up a fight, but Chase ignored her. He helped Millie pack a bag and just left with her. She was living with his family now, and that's how Chase intended to keep it.

There was no answer, so he knocked again. "Millie. Hey. Today's your dad's funeral, honey. I really think you should come," he said gently as he opened the door a crack.

"I don't want to see anyone." He could barely hear her, but at least she was talking. She hadn't said two words in the week she'd been with them.

He opened the door a little farther. "There's not going to be a lot of people there. Just me and Mar. And a few guys who worked with your dad. Less than ten. I really think you should be there to put his ashes in the ocean. He would have wanted that."

Chase turned on the light. He couldn't see her under the mound of blankets. He walked over and sat on the edge of the bed. He slowly pulled the blankets back. Her face was covered by a mess of blonde hair. He brushed some of it away, so he could see her eyes. They were red and swollen.

"Sweetie, will you please do this for me?" he said gently. He knew she would regret not saying goodbye to Mack.

She nodded slightly. "Okay."

"Do you want Mar to help you get dressed?"

She nodded again.

Chase pulled the blankets back under her chin. "She'll be up in a second."

Millie sat up after he left. She barely had the energy to do that, much less actually leave the house. She hadn't left the bed except to go to the bathroom for almost a week. Mariel came in every once in a while to deliver food that Millie barely ate. And Chase came to sit with her after she had nightmares every night. She hadn't had any human contact besides that. And now they were expecting her to talk to people at her dad's funeral. She had almost decided to change her mind about going when Mariel bounded into the room.

"Good morning, sweetie!" Mariel beamed at her. "I'm so glad you're coming with us today. It's going to be a beautiful day on the water. Some sunshine will do you good."

Mille felt exhausted just listening to her, but she tried to smile. Mariel had been so nice to her since she arrived.

"It's really hot today," Mariel said as she sorted through Millie's clothes. She had gone down to the Outer Banks yesterday and gotten more of Millie's things. Millie could imagine that Camille and Mariel had fought, but she didn't have the energy to ask about it. Mariel held up a pair of khaki shorts. "Maybe you can just wear shorts."

"No, I want to wear a dress," Millie said, pointing at the closet. "Dad really liked that pink one. He always said I looked pretty when I wore it."

Millie's eyes started to fill with tears as she slumped back down in the bed.

Mariel took the dress out of the closet and laid it on the bed. "It's beautiful, honey. That's perfect. Do you want me to help you get dressed?"

Millie looked up at her as the tears started to fall. "I don't think I can do it myself."

Mariel smoothed Millie's hair out and kissed her forehead. "Then we'll do it together. All day. It's me and you. We'll do everything together. Okay?"

Millie nodded as she wiped her tears away. "Okay."

Millie sat silently in the back seat of the car as Chase drove toward the marina. Chase told her that Mack wanted his ashes laid to rest at sea. She had to take his word for it. She had never talked to her dad about anything like that.

When they pulled up to the marina, Chase opened her door and put his arm firmly around her shoulders as they walked to the boat slip. When they got there, she saw a handful of guys that looked like Chase and her dad. She figured they were all SEALs.

As they helped her onto the boat, they introduced themselves and told her how they knew her dad. She tried to smile and nod, but she wasn't hearing anything they said. She finally made it to the bow of the boat and sat down. She felt Mariel sit down behind her and put her arms around her. They sat silently until the boat anchored a few miles off shore.

"Millie, sweetie, it's time to put your dad's ashes to rest now," Chase whispered softly into her ear. "Do you want me to do it?"

She shook her head and stood up slowly. She took the urn Chase was holding. He took the top off. She kneeled on the bench and turned the urn upside down. The ashes fell quickly into the water—some of them blowing away in the gentle wind. She watched them. All she wanted to do is dive in with them.

Chase grabbed the urn out of her hand and caught her as she started to fall forward. He hugged her tightly to his chest as she sobbed. Everything was silent around them. No one was making a sound. Millie looked up as she noticed some movement at the rear of the boat. The guys were throwing something into the ocean.

"They're throwing their tridents in after him," Chase whispered to her. "It's what we get when we become SEALs. When one of us dies, we give them our tridents as a sign of respect. Your dad was the best guy—really the absolute best among us. Always remember that."

Millie put her head back on Chase's chest as he squeezed her tighter. They sat that way all the way back to the marina.

Chapter Thirty

MILLIE, ISLAMABAD, PAKISTAN, 2020

Alex reaches across the table to hold my hand again. I know by the way he's looking at me that the wine has taken control of his body. I unfortunately remember from when we were together that wine makes him really horny.

"Millie," he says, stroking my hand with his thumb, "I've really enjoyed our dinner. Maybe we can continue this conversation with a nightcap upstairs."

I try to control the disgust that's surging through my body. We're in public, and I know I have to stay in my devoted-wife character, but he's starting to get a little too into this whole thing. It's getting creepy.

"Why don't you go up without me? I'm really full. I think I need to take a walk in the gardens to settle my stomach." I smile as I discreetly slip my hand out of his.

"I don't know if you should stay down here by yourself," he says, sitting back in his chair as the waiter hands him the dinner bill to sign. "A stroll in the gardens could be romantic."

"Actually, I could use some alone time to get my thoughts together," I say quickly. "And I'll be fine by myself. The hotel is safe." And I know Mason will stay behind to watch me. Alex still hasn't seen him. He's not nearly as sharp as he used to be, or he's just off his game because of the wine.

Alex stands up and walks around to pull out my chair. He gives me his hand to help me stand. As I get up, he puts his other arm around my waist and pulls me to him. He kisses my lips softly. It takes every ounce of self-control I have to not punch him. I push him away. He looks at me—his eyes stern like he's about to discipline me.

"PDA of any kind is inappropriate in this country. You know that," I say quietly. "And if you kiss me like that again, I will cut off your balls."

He takes a quick step back. "I'm just playing the role of your husband, Millie," he whispers thickly. He smiles and brushes my cheek with his hand. "I'll see you back up in our room."

My body shudders from revulsion as I watch him walk away. I walk quickly in the other direction. As I round the corner into the gardens, I close my eyes and inhale the sweet smell of jasmine. The fragrance is intoxicating and relaxing. Exactly what I need right now. I'm starting to relax when I hear a man clearing his throat behind me. I spin around to find a stranger standing about twenty feet from me.

"Did you know jasmine is the national flower of Pakistan?" he says, smiling.

"I didn't know that." I take a step back. "They're lovely."

"Some people say jasmine symbolizes purity and modesty, while others say it symbolizes desire and sensuality. It's mysterious—like a person with two different identities. Don't you think?"

"Maybe. I guess it depends on the person."

"I find it reminds me of a young woman—possibly born into one life, but living another—searching for her true identity."

He's testing me. He definitely wants to tell me something. "Do you know anyone like that?" I take a few steps toward him.

He smiles. "There are many young girls named after the jasmine flower. Yasmine is a very popular name in this region."

I'm within five feet of him now. The gardens are dimly lit, but I can still see his left eye twitching. "That's a beautiful name. Any girl would be lucky to have it."

"Indeed." I hear a slight quiver in his voice. "Even if she only had it for a few months after she was born."

The door to his right suddenly opens. A young couple walks out and glances at us briefly. I look back at the man. He's taken a few steps toward the door.

"Do you work at the hotel?" I ask, trying to keep him engaged, but I can see by the worried look in his eyes that the moment has passed.

He smiles and formally bows. "Mrs. Laskin, I forget myself. My apologies. My name is Mr. Bukhari. I am the manager of the hotel spa. If you are free tomorrow, I want to offer you a day at the spa as our welcome gift."

"That's so nice of you to offer. I'm not sure I have the entire day free, but I would love to come down for a treatment or two."

"As you wish," he says. "We are here to serve you. Shall we say ten in the morning to begin?"

"That sounds perfect. Thank you."

He bows quickly and disappears under the arches. I have no doubt he knows my mother named me Yasmine. Azayiz worked in the spa. Mr. Bukhari would have been her boss. He knows her. And, more importantly, he knows I'm her niece.

I'm considering what to do with this information when I'm suddenly grabbed from behind. A man wraps his arm around my chest—pinning my arms to my sides. He puts his other hand over my mouth as he pulls me out of sight under a waterfall of jasmine vines. I try to step on his foot, but he sidesteps it. I bite down hard on his finger.

"Ow." Mason's voice whispers in my ear. He lets go of me slowly.

"Mason," I whisper as I whip around to face him. "Someone's going to see us."

"No one's going to see us. I've done this before."

"What? Accosted a woman in a garden?"

"I didn't accost you," he says, smiling. "Settle down."

"Did you hear what the spa manager said to me?"

"Yeah, that's why I grabbed you. Seems like the fish are biting. He definitely was trying to send you a message."

"He knows who I am. No doubt in my mind."

"You think your aunt's going to be at your spa day tomorrow?"

"I don't know, but something's going to happen. Maybe he will give me information that gets us closer."

"Are you going to tell Alex?"

"No. Raine was right. There's something off with him. I've

never seen him so out of focus. I think I'll keep it to myself for now and see what happens tomorrow."

He nods. "We'll stay outside the spa while you're in there. Close enough that we can hear you yell if anything goes wrong."

"Okay. Are you sure you don't want to get a massage?"

He shakes his head as he starts laughing. "I've told you how I feel about strangers rubbing on my body. You rubbing on my body is another story. You think you can arrange to be my masseuse?"

"Master Chief, do you ask that of all your agents?"

"Every one of them. Even the guys."

"Well that's something we're definitely going to have to discuss when we get home," I say, smiling. "I should get back to Alex before he gets suspicious and comes looking for me."

"Babe, I'm trying to be objective, but if he kisses you again, I'm going to fucking kill him."

"Not if I kill him first. It was completely inappropriate."

"Are you sure you're safe in the same room with him?"

"Yeah," I say quietly. "He was drinking at dinner. He's never been able to hold his liquor. It makes him kind of creepy. But he's fine. He's not going to try anything. He knows I don't want it, and he hates being rejected."

"Are you going to sleep in the same bed tonight?" His tone is light, but his eyes are serious.

"I don't know. If we do, it's a king-size bed. We're not even going to touch." His eyes aren't blinking. "Mase, Alex is a lot of things, but he's not going to force himself on me. I've made it clear I'm not at all interested. He's not going to try. Even if he wants to."

"Okay." He finally blinks. "I'm just in the next room."

"I know. I've got to go."

"Agent Marsh," he says as I walk away. "I like the costume you're wearing."

I turn around to find him giving me a very appreciative once-over. "It's not a costume, you weirdo. It's traditional dress for this region."

"I definitely think you should bring it home. Maybe you can wear it when you're giving me the massage."

"Stop," I say, laughing as I duck under the jasmine vines and out into the night.

Chapter Thirty-One

MASON, ISLAMABAD, PAKISTAN, 2020

"Mase," Bryce says as he shoves my shoulder hard, waking me up instantly from my light sleep.

I leap off the bed and grab my pistol from the nightstand. "What's wrong? Is Millie okay?"

"I'm not sure. We heard what we thought was her yelling. Ty went in and found Alex on top of her, trying to pin her down."

I'm already across the suite and through the adjoining room door. Ty has Alex pressed up against the wall. Alex is wearing pajama bottoms, but no shirt. Millie—fully dressed in sweatpants and my fleece—is rocking back and forth with her head in her hands.

"She was having a bad dream!" Alex shouts at Ty and then turns to look at me. "I was just trying to wake her up. She was having a nightmare. I wasn't trying to attack her. Are you fucking kidding me? I was trying to wake her up."

I point at Alex. "Out of the room. Now."

"This is ridiculous," he says as Ty pushes him roughly toward the other room.

"Does he get to live or not?" Ty pauses at the door and looks back at me.

I tilt Millie's face up and see the anguished eyes she always has after she has a nightmare about her dad. "Yeah. He can live. He didn't attack her. Just keep him in that room for the rest of the night. No one comes back in here," I say without taking my eyes off Millie.

I hear the door click behind me as I gently sit down on the bed next to her.

"Hey," I say as I start to rub her back.

She looks up at me. The tears start welling up as her head collapses down on my shoulder.

I pull her to my chest and whisper in her ear, "Which one was it?"

"The one where the house blows up and his body's flying toward me and he's yelling my name," she says, sobbing into my shoulder. "Why do I keep having these nightmares? Why can't they end?"

"I don't know, baby. But it's over now," I say, pulling her onto my lap and rocking her gently against my chest. "I'm here. I'm not going anywhere."

I kiss the top of her head lightly as I whisper over and over, "I've got you. I've got you." Her breathing finally starts to slow down a little bit.

She looks up at me with her sad eyes. "Will you stay here with me tonight?"

"All night. I'll be here all night. Go back to sleep now, Mills. I'm right here."

I lay her down gently and pull the blankets over her. I pull her body tightly to me. "You're okay," I whisper until she slips back into sleep.

I'm awake most of the night, waiting for another night-mare to try to attack her. I'm on full alert—ready to beat it back to whatever subconscious hell-hole it's trying to escape. It never comes. She opens her eyes as the sun starts shining through the curtains. She looks a little confused when she sees me, but then smiles.

"Hey," she says with such familiarity that I think for a second we're back in San Diego, ready to make out for a while before we grab our morning coffee.

"Hey. Did you sleep okay?" I pull her a little closer before she remembers where we are and tries to pull away.

She pushes her body closer to mine. "Yeah, I didn't have any more nightmares."

"Mills, do you think this all is a little bit too much for you? We can go home any time you want."

She breathes in deeply. "I have to at least try to find Azayiz—ask what she knows about Dad."

"Okay," I say slowly. "Are you ready to tell me the rest of the story yet?"

She rolls over and looks at me. "Do you think this room is bugged?"

"Not a chance. We sweep it every time you leave the room. It's clean. We looked in Alex's gear, too. Did you know he's carrying a Glock?"

"No, I didn't. He told me we weren't allowed to carry on this mission."

"That figures. We'll deal with that later. Will you please tell me what I don't know?"

She takes a deep breath and slowly exhales. "So when Chase and I met with George the other day, he repeated that Dad had asked him to help him disappear. George said he called his boss right after Dad left his office. His boss told him that he would handle it from there and ordered George to back off. His boss at the time was Paul Ward who—as you know—is the director now. When George told us the director had taken over my dad's request, I told him I wanted to meet with Ward to find out what he knew. I didn't think there was any chance in hell they would grant the meeting, but they did. I was headed to meet with Ward within an hour of my request."

"Did Chase go with you?"

"Yeah. He went all the way to the outer office, but Ward and I met alone. Ward told me they had staged Dad's death. He escaped the explosion through a tunnel. Agents met him in the tunnel and took him to a meeting spot."

"You believe this?"

She rolls over on her back and looks up at the ceiling. "I do. He was telling the truth. I don't have a doubt in my mind that Dad was alive after the explosion."

"You're the best at reading people, so I'll believe you. Where did they say they hid him after that?"

"They didn't. The agency only agreed to do anything because Azayiz asked them to. Ward made it very clear Dad wasn't at all important to him. They only did this because Azayiz had helped them with the bin Laden raid. She was apparently the key informant. That's why she had to go into hiding."

"So what happened when your dad hit the end of the tunnel? You said they took him to a meeting spot. Who'd he meet?"

"Ward said Azayiz had arranged for someone to meet him in Baghdad. He said they handed Dad off and didn't ask questions. They washed their hands of it after that."

"So they could have been handing him to the enemy?"

"Yep." She closes her eyes for a second. A tear rolls down her cheek. "I said I believed he didn't blow up in the building that day, but I think he's dead. He could have died later that day or a year after that, but he would never stay away from me this long. Never."

I take a deep breath. "I love you with everything in me. And I have no problem believing it's still only half as much as your dad loved you. If someone told me today my being around you was threatening your life, I would disappear forever so that you could live. It would be the hardest decision I'd ever make in my life, but I would do it in a second. I can only imagine your dad would have done that and more."

She turns and looks at me again. "There's one more thing. Apparently, Dad made a deal with the agency that if they helped him, he would never resurface. He had to stay away forever. They basically wiped his identity clean—took his passport, erased all mentions of him in naval records, probably destroyed every trace of him."

"That would explain him staying away for so long."

"Yeah, and apparently he at least made it to Baghdad after the explosion. Raine found the guy Dad's team used as a translator back in the day—an Iraqi national. She and Chase are there now. They talked to him yesterday. He confirmed he helped with the meeting with Azayiz's people."

"Raine's with Chase?"

"Yeah. That was part of my deal with Ward. He said he'd support Chase and Raine going to Iraq and retracing Dad's movement from that side."

I take her hand gently. "I don't mean to insult you, but there's no way in the world the director of the CIA is doing all this for a 25-year-old agent—much less an agent who tried to resign from the agency. There's something way bigger than you and your dad going on here."

"Oh, I'm aware. This has nothing to do with appeasing me. It has everything to do with finding Azayiz. There's something really suspicious going on with her disappearance. I'm just not sure what it is yet."

"Is that everything?"

"Chase said the translator told him the people they met in Baghdad were from Pakistan, but they were speaking a Dardic language. He thinks it was Kalasha."

"Why's that important?"

"There aren't many people who still speak that language. Raine did some research," she says, pausing for second. "She found out Azayiz's grandmother was from the Kalasha Valley. She still has family near Birir. If she helped Dad escape, he could be hiding there. It's kind of the perfect place to hide—remote, cloistered."

"Yeah, but from what I've read, they aren't much into outsiders. I can't imagine they would be okay with an American hiding out there, especially for nine years. I don't think that's very likely. Plus, it's so close to the Afghanistan border and the FATA. It's not like it's completely safe. Even if he got there, surely someone would have given him up to the Taliban or worse."

"I don't think we're that far yet," she says. "Chase believes the Iraqi guy. He thinks Dad made it to Baghdad. He doesn't know what happened after that. He and Raine are headed to Birir right now."

I reach for her hand as we both look up at the ceiling. We lie there silently for a few minutes.

"So you think he's still alive?" She says it so quietly, I can barely hear her.

I squeeze her hand. "I don't know, Mills. I really don't. But for the first time, I think it's possible."

Chapter Thirty-Two

MILLIE, ISLAMABAD, PAKISTAN, 2020

Mason and I are still snuggling silently in bed when a loud rap on the adjoining room door brings us out of our thoughts. The door opens a crack.

"Mase," Bryce says.

"You can come in," Mason says without removing his arm from around me.

Bryce peeks his head in carefully. When he sees we're decent, he opens the door further. "Alex is whining that he needs to get to a golf game or something. He says he needs to get ready. I can tell him to shut the fuck up again if you want me to."

"No, it's fine," Mason says, standing up and pulling me up with him.

Bryce steps aside and motions Alex through the door. Alex glares at Mason.

"I need to change, and I'm going to order breakfast for

us," Alex says, motioning to me. "Would you please go back to your room, Master Chief?"

"Naw, I'm good here," Mason says, sitting on the couch.

"Millie and I both have appointments this morning. We need to get ready," Alex says, pointing to the door.

"Knock yourself out. I won't look." Mason looks down at his phone.

Before Alex can say anything else, I grab my toiletry bag and a change of clothes. "I'll go first," I say as I head to the bathroom.

When I come out, Mason is gone, but the rooms' adjoining door is still open. Alex is sitting at the table eating breakfast— newly changed into his golf clothes.

"Join me for breakfast," he says, waving his hand over the top of the display of food.

"I'll at least have some coffee," I say, glancing quickly through the adjoining room's doorway as I walk by. Mason's coming back through it. "Do you guys need some breakfast? It looks like Alex ordered enough for all of us."

"We're good. We'll eat when he leaves." Much to Alex's annoyance, Mason sits back down on the couch in our room.

"Millie, come in here for a second." I hear Ty's voice booming from the other room. "My wife sent me pictures of my daughter's birthday party. You have to see them."

First of all, Ty doesn't have a wife or a daughter. Second, if he did, he would never show me—or anyone—pictures of a kid's birthday party. I look at Mason, but he's focused on his phone like nothing unusual is happening. I'm guessing there's something they want to show me without involving Alex.

"Aww, I want to see them," I say with the appropriate

amount of fake enthusiasm. Alex stares at me coldly as I walk into the other room.

I barely clear the threshold when Bryce pulls me behind the door. He grabs me under the arms and lifts me off the floor —one of his hands firmly covering my mouth. Butch grabs my left leg, shoving my skirt up as he slides a garter holster up to my thigh. He takes a .38 revolver out of his waistband and puts it in the holster. Bryce places me back on the ground gently.

Ty holds up five fingers. "Can you believe she's only five? I know she looks a lot bigger, but she's only five."

I nod. I'm not sure why they've just force-armed me with a gun, but I've got it. Five rounds. "She really does look bigger. I can't believe she's only five. She's adorable."

I walk back into my room just as Alex is walking by the door. "You said your spa appointment is at ten? I'll walk you down there on my way out."

"I want to finish my coffee first. You can go without me."

"I don't mind waiting," he says a little too loudly.

I know he wants to talk to me alone, and he's going to be persistent about it. "Okay. Give me a few minutes."

He paces by the door as I manage to get down a little food and two cups of coffee. I grab my bag.

Mason looks up from his phone. "Agent Laskin, do you want any protection today?"

"No," Alex says. "And Agent Marsh doesn't need it, either."

Mason smiles at me. I know he'll be outside the spa like he said he would.

As the room door closes behind us, Alex grabs my wrist

and pulls me to the elevators. "All of that," he says, waving his hand back toward our room. "All of that last night was completely inappropriate. First, you come back in the room after dinner smelling like him. What if someone had seen you two together in public? Then you spend the night with him in our room? You've lost your goddamn mind if you think that's appropriate behavior for an agent on assignment."

I break his hold on my wrist as the elevator door opens. "Let's just get through the rest of this," I hiss. "I'll let you know if I learn any more at the spa today. You can take the next elevator."

His eyes bore into me until the elevator closes. The last thing I feel like doing right now is getting a massage, but I push the button for the spa level anyway.

As I walk out of the elevator, I see Butch sitting at a table at the top of the staircase that leads down to the spa. As I walk by him, he whispers, "Keep your phone in your hand during your massage." I nod and start down the staircase.

Mr. Bukhari is at the spa's check-in desk when I walk in. There's no one else in the room.

"Mrs. Laskin, I'm so glad you could join us," he says, bowing his head slightly. "Will you follow me to our waiting room?"

I smile and follow him through a doorway that leads to what looks like empty treatment rooms. I don't see anyone— not even spa workers. It's really quiet. We walk past all the rooms and through a doorway that looks like an exit back into the hotel.

"If you will wait here, someone will help you shortly. Please help yourself to some tea or water," he says, waving his arm toward what looks like a hastily set up drink bar. He smiles as he backs out of the room.

I turn around. The room is big—at least 2,500 square feet. It looks more like a small conference room than a spa waiting room. There are three doors including the one we just walked through. I open the door to my right. It's a supply closet. As I walk toward the other door, it opens slowly. A woman— wearing a scarf around her head—walks in. When she looks up and sees me, she slowly lowers the scarf onto her shoulders. Her eyes widen as she looks at me. She shakes her head as a slight smile comes to her face.

"You look just like her," she says softly.

"Several people have told me that," I say, smiling back at her. "I'm assuming you're my aunt Azayiz."

She walks slowly to me and reaches out to gently touch my face. "You can call me Aza, Yasmine." Her tired eyes light up slightly as she says my name. "Although I should call you Millie. That's your name now."

"You can call me Yasmine if you like. It's a pretty name. I understand it was my grandma's name."

"It was. She was a strong, beautiful woman. When Nejra found out she was pregnant, she so wanted it to be a girl, so she could name you after her mother," she says, looking down. "Nejra's life ended the day her parents died and began again the day you were born. She would have been such a good mother. She wanted to be your mother with everything inside her."

"I'm sorry I never got a chance to know her. My father told me she was very special."

She looks back up at me. "I'm glad he realized that. Her

life changed forever when she met him. I wish she had not engaged with him, but she was drawn to him like a moth to the flames. At least she knew great passion. Do you know that passion with your husband?"

"I'm not married," I say as she nods her head.

"It is what I thought. My son, Fareed, told me that you worked for the CIA. You met him a few months ago when you met your uncle Sayid. So this was all a trap to take me back into custody? It's what Fareed said to expect."

"I'm not going to take you anywhere you don't want to go. I just want to know if my dad's alive. Do you know?"

She breathes in deeply as she turns to walk toward a row of chairs. She sits down and looks up at me. "Do you know your husband—or I guess your partner agent—is the person who gave up my hiding location?"

"What?" I say as my mind starts spinning. "Alex?"

"Yes. The agency hid me successfully for nine years until he became the head of this region. He sold me out within a month of having the job. I'm still not sure why."

I shake my head and look down. I can't believe he would do that, but it's starting to make sense now why he wants her back so badly. He's promised her to someone, and if he's not able to deliver, he's probably going to be killed.

"I'm sorry he did that. I had no idea. Do you know who he told about you?"

"Fareed said one of the government ministers told them where my safe house was. I barely got out before they got there. I've been hiding with friends since then."

"So Fareed has been playing both sides? For how long?"

"Since I moved back to Pakistan. Your uncle Sayid was

like his big brother. Fareed was loyal to him, but he's more loyal to his mother. He fed me information about the network for years. Sadly, he would never give me their location. This could have been over long ago if he had."

"You're putting yourself in danger by coming here today."

She smiles. "I would do anything to see you. I'm sure your agency knows that. It was a good plan to get me out of hiding."

"Thank you," Alex says from the corner of the room. I whip my head around to see him walking toward us with his Glock pointed at Aza.

"Alex, put the gun down," I say as I try to discreetly reach under my skirt for my gun. His eyes are focused on her. "Alex. Put it down. She's not armed."

"You think I'm going to trust you? Who's your allegiance to, Millie? It's definitely not to me," Alex says.

His eyes dart briefly to me. They're wild and unfocused. "Alex, I'm completely on your side. We have a job to do here. Let's just take her back into protective custody. Our mission is successful."

"I heard everything she said to you," he says, his eyes still fixed on Aza. "She told you I turned her in. That's true. Part of my job is to redevelop a relationship with the Pakistan govern-ment. All they want is her, and we'll be in good standing with them again. That's when my mission will be successful."

"Alex, put the gun down. I'm not going to ask again." He looks over to me and sees my gun pointed at him.

"Are you going to shoot me, Millie? Really? You've never shot anything in your life except a paper target. It's different when the target's breathing. You don't have what it takes. I knew it the minute I met you. That's why you've never gotten in the field. You shouldn't be here now, but you did manage to get your aunt to come out of hiding, so I guess you did one thing right."

Aza's curled up on the floor with her hands over her head. She looks up at him as he stands above her and says, "They wanted to kill you, but I don't think they'll mind too much if I do it."

As his finger begins to slide to the trigger, I fire a shot— hitting him purposely in the leg. I want to give him another chance to put his gun down. The force spins him around to face me. He lifts his arms to fire at me. I fire another round— hitting him in his forehead. He falls to the ground, blood shooting out of his head. I walk slowly toward him with my gun still drawn. I kick his gun out of his hand and lean down to check his pulse. I already know he's dead. I take a long, shaky breath as I lean over to close his eyes. I let my hand linger on his chest for a second before I force myself to look away.

Aza's covered in his blood—her eyes wide with shock. I kneel down to look in her face.

"Do you know if my dad is alive?" I say, touching her shoulder to try to get her to focus.

She's shaking. I can tell she's finding it hard to speak. She shakes her head slightly. "No," she whispers.

"If he's alive, do you know where he might be?"

"Yes," she says more loudly. "I arranged for my cousin to take him to my grandparents' house in the Kalasha Valley. I don't know if they made it there. I don't know if he's alive.

But if he's alive, he might be there or have been there at one time."

"Can you take me there?"

She nods as I help her up. Her eyes go over my shoulder to look at something. I turn around to see Mr. Bukhari looking at Alex's body. He turns to me, his eyes wide as he looks at the gun in my hand.

"He's on my side," Aza says quietly from behind me.

I reach into my pocket and turn off the recorder on my cell phone. I type a text message to Mason, but don't hit send. I hand the phone to Mr. Bukhari.

"A very large, angry man with a beard is going to come through your doors within the hour. Give him this phone. Don't call the authorities until he gets here. Do you understand?"

He nods and reaches out to take Aza's hand. "Good luck, my friend," he says in Pashto. She nods and smiles.

"Let's go, Millie," she says. "We have a long drive ahead of us."

Chapter Thirty-Three

MASON, ISLAMABAD, PAKISTAN, 2020

Millie hasn't contacted me since she went into the spa. I asked her to text me at least once an hour. It's been almost ninety minutes. She's either blissed out from her massage or something's wrong.

"Stay here," I say to Butch. "I'm going to check on her."

As I descend the spiral staircase to the spa welcome area, the man at the desk eyes me suspiciously. It's the same guy from the gardens last night. I put my hand on my pistol still concealed in the back of my waistband.

"Good afternoon, sir," he says as I reach the bottom of the stairs. "I'm sorry, but our spa is closed for the day. Perhaps you will come back tomorrow."

"I'm here to check on my wife. She came for a massage around ten and hasn't left yet," I say, looking toward the door behind him.

"That's quite impossible, sir. The spa has been closed all day."

I pull my gun out. "Open the door."

"There is no one inside, sir," he says, his voice beginning to shake.

I walk around the desk, grab him, and shove him toward the door. "Open the door now or I shoot off the lock."

As he pulls out his keys, I call Butch. "There's something wrong. Call JJ. Get them over here immediately with all the supplies. Get Ty and Bryce down to the valet to see if they saw Millie leave. Have Base track her phone and then get down here."

The spa's empty and quiet as we enter. I pat the man down. He's not armed. I keep him in front of me and make him start opening treatment room doors. We're three doors in when Butch comes charging through. I throw the man to him and clear the rest of the rooms quickly. When I get to the end of the rooms, I see an exit door.

"What's through here?" I say, looking back at the man.

He doesn't say anything. Butch puts his gun to the man's head. "What's in there?" Butch demands.

"A dead body," the man whispers.

I kick open the door with my gun drawn. I see a man's body to my right. It's Alex. He's lying face-up—shot in the forehead. And as I get closer I see a leg wound.

"Looks like the head shot is a .38 round from at least twenty feet away," Butch says from behind me. "Definitely Millie's gun. Either her or someone disarmed her. It's dead-center in his forehead. Can she make that shot?"

"Yeah," I say, taking a deep breath to try to clear my head. "She can."

My phone rings. It's Culver.

"Give me a sit rep now," he says before I can say anything.

"Agent Laskin is dead—back room of the hotel spa. Agent Marsh isn't here. Where's her cellphone?"

"It's showing in the hotel."

"Butch," I say, looking at him. He's already slammed the man against the wall.

"Where's her cellphone?" he yells, his pistol pressed firmly against the man's head.

The man starts to reach into his pocket. Butch grabs his arm and pins it back to the wall. He reaches in the man's pocket and pulls out a cellphone. He tosses it to me.

"We found her cellphone," I say to Culver. "She's not with it."

I type in her passcode. The screen opens to an unsent text message to me.

I'm going to find my dad with Azayiz. She thinks he was in the Kalasha Valley at some point. Meet us there. Sorry I went without you. She can't be taken back into U.S. custody. Watch my last video. I'll call you as soon as I can. I love you.

"There's a message from her. It says she's going to find her dad," I say to Culver. "Call Chase and see if he's gotten any closer to where that might be."

"JJ should be almost at the hotel. Get geared up and get to the airport," Culver says. "I'll have a helo meet you there."

"Roger that."

205

I grab the man from Butch. "If she's dead, I'm coming back for you," I say as I throw him to the ground.

As we head to the lobby, I watch the video. Her phone must have still been in her pocket because the picture is black, but the audio's clear. It's a play-by-play of how Alex died. I fucking knew he was the one who gave up Azayiz's position.

I only hear two shots on the recording. Both sound like a .38, so Alex likely didn't get any shots off before Millie took him down. I know she shot him in the leg to give him another chance to surrender. That pisses me off so badly. She knows better than that. If she's alive, I'm definitely going to lecture her about taking a kill shot first.

As Butch and I get to the lobby, we see our team fully loaded standing outside waiting for us. The hotel manager rushes over to me.

"We did not agree to this! Please have them put their weapons away. They're scaring our guests," he says, tugging at my arm.

I grab him by his collar. "You have a dead body in your spa. Worry about that."

He gasps as I throw him away from me.

"They have her cellphone tracked?" JJ says as we walk out to them. "No one here saw her leave."

"You mean this cellphone?" I hold it up as I grab a vest and a rifle.

He pulls out his cellphone and shows me a map. "I put a GPS tracker on her leg holster before I packed it back in Virginia because I knew she'd pull some high-maintenance shit like this. I'm guessing she's wearing it?"

I nod. "Yeah. Where is she?"

"Not the strongest signal. Last ping I got was just this side of Peshawar. Looks like she might be headed north. That mean anything to you?"

"Yeah. That's the way to the Kalasha Valley."

Chapter Thirty-Four

CHASE, KALASHA VALLEY, PAKISTAN, 2020

"Are you sure they said it was that house?" I ask Raine as we peer at the house from behind a wall.

"I think. I don't speak Kalasha. The one guy who spoke a little bit of Urdu said the American lived in this house. But I also gave him a big wad of cash, so there's a really good chance he was lying."

As I consider our options, one of my grandma's sayings pops into my mind: "If you win, you will be happy; if you lose, you will be wise." In my current predicament, I figure I can replace the word "wise" with "dead."

"Stay here, Raine," I say as I start around the wall. "If anything happens to me, leave me here. Get to a satellite-friendly area and call Culver."

When I get within fifty feet of the house, I see the butt of a rifle poke out through a window. All I can think about is how mad Mariel's going to be if I die. I stop, pull down the scarf from my face, and put my hands slowly in the air.

"My name is Chase Taylor. I'm looking for a man named Mack Marsh."

There's a long pause before I hear a familiar voice. "I know what your name is, dumbass. What I can't figure out is how you found me."

When I hear his voice—for the first time in nine years—a weird mixture of anger and relief rockets through my body. I put my arms down and watch in shock as the door opens and my best friend walks out. He still looks pretty much the same.

"I don't know whether to kiss you or kill you," I say as I put my pistol back in my waistband.

"Your choice," Mack says, walking down the stairs. "But I'm definitely going to fight you on either one."

I grab him into a hug. We stand there for a good minute, not saying anything. This is by far the longest hug we've ever shared.

"Please tell me Millie's okay," he finally says. I push him back roughly.

"What the fuck, Mack? How could you do this to her?" I say as my anger starts to rise. "How could you do this to me?"

Mack looks down. "You don't know the whole story."

"I actually think I do know it now, but frankly, it doesn't come close to helping me understand. Do you have any idea what you did to her?"

"I saved her life." Mack looks back up at me with his infamous glare.

I glare back at him. "You took away her life when you died —or disappeared or whatever the fuck you did. And you left me to pick up the pieces. What the fuck?"

Mack's eyes shift quickly behind me. I turn to see Raine walking toward us—her hands in the air.

"Is she with you?" Mack asks.

"Yeah. Put your hands down, Raine."

"What happened to Mariel?" Mack asks.

"She's not my wife, asshole. She's a CIA agent. By the way, so is your daughter. Do you even know that about her?"

Mack takes a step back. "What? Millie works for the CIA?"

"Yeah. So much for not wanting her in this life. You drove her right to it. Have you not even been keeping up with what she's doing?"

"Do you see where I'm living? There's no internet service up here. I haven't had any news of her or anything else since I left. Honestly, I haven't really wanted to. It would have been too painful."

I shake my head. "I thought I knew you better than anyone on earth, but I don't get you at all right now."

"Do you want to come in and let me explain?" he says, gesturing toward the house.

"There's nothing you can say to me that's going to help me understand but, yeah, we'll come in."

I step aside and motion Raine ahead of me. I take a quick look around before I follow them into the very small, two-room house.

"So what? You've been living in this shack for the past nine years?"

"Yeah."

"How, Mack?" I say as I look around at the sparse accommodations.

"You know it doesn't take much to make me comfortable." Mack pulls out a chair from the table for Raine to sit down. Raine smiles at him.

"My name is Raine. Millie's a close friend of mine. She's told me all about you."

Mack looks at her without blinking. "She talks about me?"

"Nonstop," Raine says, declining the chair and moving back toward the door. "Although everything Chase said is true —Millie still loves you so much. You're the only reason she did any of this over the past year. I'm going to give you two a chance to catch up. I'll be outside."

Mack looks back at me. "What did Millie do over the past year?"

"It's too long of a story and we don't have time right now. We have a SEAL team incoming. You need to get ready to move."

"What? What's happening? How did you even know I was alive?"

"Millie found you. She's in Islamabad right now looking for her aunt Azayiz, who I believe helped you escape."

"How did Millie find out about Azayiz?" Mack asks, his face twisted with confusion.

"It's a long story, Mack. Really. It's too much for right now. Do you have anything you need to pack or whatever?"

"I can't leave, Chase. I'm not allowed back in the U.S."

"I know about all the conditions you agreed to, but you're coming back. I don't care if I have to knock you out and carry you. You go to jail if you have to, but you're coming back with us. At least Millie can visit you in jail."

Mack takes a deep breath, his eyes shifting back and forth

across the room. "Is Millie with them? The team that's coming in?"

"I don't know. The last real satellite reception we got was in Gabhirat. Raine found Azayiz's family home and told Culver that's where we were headed. He's sending some helos in to grab us."

"Culver? Harry Culver?"

I laugh. "Yeah. He's a captain now—in charge of all the teams in Virginia Beach."

"That seriously might be the most shocking thing you've said yet," Mack says, shaking his head.

Raine walks back in. "Chase," she says, holding up her binoculars, "I think we have incoming to the north."

I grab my pistol out of my waistband. Mack grabs my arm and opens a closet door. It's full of weapons and ammunition.

"What's this?" I ask him, admiring the small arsenal.

He hands me an old-body AK. "That's too long of a story, too. Let's just say, I haven't been sitting on my ass these last nine years," he says, smiling. "I've got kind of a ham radio setup here too, if you think you can use it to get to Culver."

"Do you know how to do that?" I say, looking at Raine.

"Yeah, I can figure it out," she says, grabbing the radio out of the closet.

I take her binoculars and look out the window. I see the movement to the north. It looks like team movement. "I think it's our guys, but just to be sure," I say, lining up my rifle on the window sill.

Mack settles in at the only other window. We wait for a few minutes until we can see the movement more clearly. The leader holds up his hand to stop the approach.

"Chase!" I hear Mason yell.

"Yeah, man. We've got you covered the rest of the way. Door's on the south side," I say as I go outside to greet them.

Chapter Thirty-Five

MILLIE, KALASHA VALLEY, PAKISTAN, 2020

"What do you mean she jumped off the wall?" I ask, laughing.

"I mean she said she was a princess warrior, spread her arms like wings, and jumped." Aza glances at me, her face glowing. "Three meters later, she is lying at the bottom of the wall—wailing—holding her broken leg."

"Oh, poor thing. I'm sure it hurt." I'm trying to imagine what my mom looked like at the bottom of that wall.

"Her father tried to scold her as he was picking her up to take her to the hospital. He was smiling though. He secretly loved her independence. She was one of his only weaknesses."

I take a deep breath as my heart drops. It seems like I have something else in common with my mom. Aza reaches over to hold my hand for at least the tenth time. In the past three hours on our drive, I've heard story after story about my mom. It's been lovely and painful. After every story, Aza asks me if she should go on. I want her to go on forever.

She squeezes my hand and lets go. "We are getting close to

the valley. There will likely be guards at some point along the road. The Kalasha do not much like outsiders. Climb into the back seat and wrap your scarf around your head until only your eyes are showing. I will tell them you are my guest to visit my family. Try not to say anything to them. Don't speak in Pashto. We don't want to let them know you understand it. Only speak English or Urdu."

"I only know a little bit of Urdu," I say, climbing into the back seat.

"English is fine. Your accent would give you away anyway."

When we turn off the main road in Gabhirat toward the Birir Valley, the roads—if that's what you can call them—get steeper and much skinnier. Aza's driving them like a pro, but I'm still half convinced we're going to go off the side of the mountain. As much as I want to hear more stories about Mom, I decide to keep quiet and let Aza concentrate on driving. My mind just has a second to think about what I might find at the end of this road when I see a guard station ahead of us.

Aza pulls up next to the guard and speaks to him in a language I don't understand. I'm assuming it's Kalasha. He points back to me a few times. I look down at the floorboard to make sure Alex's Glock hasn't slipped out of its hiding place under the passenger's seat. It hasn't. My .38 is still strapped to my leg. I've already checked the mag on the Glock —15 rounds, two spent. With both guns, I have sixteen rounds. I've never shot a Glock, but I'm guessing I can still get a shot in this guy's head from two feet away.

Aza reaches into her dress and pulls out a roll of cash. She gives the guard the entire roll and we're on our way. I don't even ask who the guard was. I'm guessing he's friendly to the Kalasha people with the respect he showed Aza. He's not a threat. I'm guessing our threats lie ahead as we wind our way closer to the Afghanistan border.

When we finally start descending into the Kalasha Valley, the scene takes my breath away. The emerald green valley with snow-capped mountains behind it reminds me of a Swiss village. There's a beautiful crystal-blue river running through the town. As we get closer, I see tiny wooden houses built into the foothills. We stop at one of them.

"My grandparents' house," Aza says as she turns and smiles at me. "My son lives here now. Let's go in. Remember only English. We don't want anyone to know you understand Pashto."

I take a deep breath. I'm hoping she has a secret son no one knows about, but I'm guessing we're talking about Fareed —the man who kidnapped me with Yusef Hadzic. This would be the perfect location for him. It's just east of the Hindu Kush. He could have gone easily between wherever Sayid's network was hiding in the mountains to this house. I decide quickly not to bring the Glock. I don't have a good place to hide it. My .38 has three rounds. I hope it's enough.

The door to the house is so short that I have to duck to get in. When I straighten up, I see Fareed sitting at a rickety kitchen table. There's a teapot hanging over the small fire in the fireplace to his left. A mattress takes up what's left of the room. He's alone, and he's staring right at me.

"Hi, Fareed," I say as calmly as possible. "I haven't seen you since you kidnapped me a few months back. I hope you've been well."

He doesn't smile. Apparently, my sarcasm is lost on him. He turns to Aza and says in Pashto, "Why is she here?"

"She is my niece and your cousin. She's here to visit," Aza says, not looking at him. She gets two small cups off the counter and motions for me to sit on the other chair at the table as she pours me a cup of tea.

"Was I right about her trying to trap you for the CIA?" Fareed says in Pashto.

"You were right that it was the plan, but she helped me escape. She's working both sides of the equation. You know something about that." Aza goes to the fire to warm her hands. Fareed doesn't reply to her last statement.

"So it looks like neither one of us died in Sarajevo. Are you looking to finish the job this time?" I say to Fareed, still speaking in English, as instructed by Aza.

His eyes narrow as his stare becomes more aggressive. "I saved your life that day," he says.

"Really? That's not how I remember it. I remember you putting a hood over my head and shoving me into a car."

"Yusef wanted to kill you right there on the road. I stopped him from doing that and got you to your uncle Sayid. I knew he wouldn't kill you."

My mind goes back to that day as I suddenly remember Fareed yelling at Yusef to not touch me. I also remember him handling me as gently as he could under the circumstances.

"Why didn't you let him kill me?"

"Because Sayid wanted to see you—again—before he died. He hadn't seen you since your dad took you when you were only a few months old."

"How did you escape the house when the SEAL team arrived?"

"Just like your dad did—through a tunnel."

Aza stands behind him now, shaking her head—her eyes fixed on me. I'm guessing by her panicked look, I shouldn't mention we're here to look for Dad. I look back at Fareed.

"How did you know to get in the tunnel? How did you know they were coming?"

"Why do you think I didn't search you? I knew you had a phone. Sayid wanted them to rescue you. He was going to kill Yusef and himself that day no matter what. He wanted you to get out."

"Why didn't Yusef search me?"

"Because he was as dumb as a chicken."

"All the other men in the house died."

"We had to make it look real." He shrugs. "With Sayid gone, I had no interest in carrying on with the network. He asked me, and I said no. We made the plan that everyone had to die except for me and hopefully you."

He sees the confused look on my face.

"You were his niece. You are my cousin," he says. "We both loved Nejra. You were a baby. You had no fault for what happened. Your dad, on the other hand . . ."

My mind finally goes back to my dad. That's why I'm here. I don't expect to find him, but I need to know.

"How long have you lived here?" I ask Fareed.

"Only a few days. I lived in the mountains with the network most of the time. I went to visit Mom in Islamabad before she went into hiding. I was—how do you say it?—a vagabond. When Mom called me and told me she was hoping to move here, I came down from the mountains."

"Yes, and I'm glad Millie could be our first guest," Aza says. "I'm going to take her up the road to show her some of the other houses. We'll be back soon."

She looks at me and nods toward the door. I stand up.

Fareed says in Pashto, "Why are you going up there? You just got here after a long trip. What's going on, Momma?"

"Nothing is going on," Aza replies in Pashto. "She's enchanted by the valley and wants to see more of it. And there used to be a boarding-house up that way. Do you think she's going to stay here and sleep on the mattress with us?"

"I'll go with you," he says as he stands up.

"That's not necessary," she says quickly.

"Momma, there are people looking for you. They have to know you will try to hide here. I need to protect you." He walks over to a small closet and pulls out a rifle.

I look in the closet quickly before he closes the door. That seems to be the only rifle available. I'll have to stick to my pistols. We walk out to Aza's car.

"I'll drive," I say, trying to gain some control over where we go next.

"You're bossy like Nejra was," Fareed says to me. "I'll drive. Get in the back seat."

At least I'll have easier access to the Glock from the back seat. I get in and push my foot under the seat. I glide the Glock toward me until I can see the barrel.

I look up as we start driving. Aza's giving him directions in Pashto. She tells him to drive to a house—that she says is the boarding-house—about a mile up on the left. As we get onto the road, I hear gunfire behind us. I turn around to look out the back window just as it shatters.

I see at least ten men running toward us—still about a hundred feet out. I look back to Fareed as he slams the accelerator into the floor—throwing me against Aza's seat. I grab the Glock as I'm falling and somehow duck down as another round comes in through the back window. I see blood splatter all over the car as I hear Fareed yell "Momma!" in Bosnian.

He grabs for her as the car spins out of control, finally coming to a rest as he slams on the brakes. I crawl out of the car and peek around it. The men—armed with rifles—are still coming at us. Fareed pulls Aza out of the car and tries to stop the bleeding from her head. She's obviously dead, but he keeps trying. I grab his rifle and start firing at the men. I have two down quickly. They take cover, but I know it's only going to be a matter of minutes before they realize how lightly armed we are.

Chapter Thirty-Six

MASON, KALASHA VALLEY, PAKISTAN, 2020

When we get to the airport, the helo is ready for takeoff. Culver walks down the ramp of the transport plane toward me. I've never seen his face look like this. It's a weird combination of happy and pissed off.

"What?" I say when he gets within five feet of me.

He grabs my arm and pulls me away from the team. "Mack is alive," he says quietly.

"Millie's dad? You can't be serious."

He nods his head slowly—looking like he only half believes it himself. "Chase found him. He's in the Birir Valley. Apparently, he's been there the whole time."

I take a deep breath, shaking my head. "Millie's headed that way. JJ put a tracker on a leg holster we brought for her. Unreliable signal, but he got a ping headed north just east of Peshawar."

"She's with her aunt?"

"Apparently. Not sure if the signal's strong enough to isolate her for a vehicle intervention on the road."

"Yeah," he says. "We couldn't do that anyway that close to the FATA. If we did, we'd have to grab her and get out of the country. I'm guessing she's not going to want to go."

"I could force her, but I'm not sure that's the best thing for any of us right now. I swear to God, if she gets killed before she sees him or vice versa, I'm going to fucking lose it."

"That's not going to happen. Get your head in the game and get up to Birir."

"My head is firmly in the game."

"The birds aren't going to be able to stay in the region for long. Too close to the Hindu Kush. Lots of heat-seeking missiles in that area. You have to get in and out as quickly as possible. And just so you know, your official mission is to get Chase, Mack, and Raine and meet us at the base in Jalalabad. The agency has officially called off the hunt for Azayiz Custovic, and anyone else who might be with her."

I glare at him. "I understand what my official mission is, sir."

He nods and pats me on the shoulder. "Glad you understand, Master Chief," he says and then whispers, "If you leave that valley without her, I'll shoot you myself."

"Roger that," I say as I head to the helo.

We land in the valley west of the house where Chase and Raine are apparently with Millie's dad. I'm still not fully believing he's alive. We hoof it about a half mile and close in on the back of the house. I see two rifle barrels pointed at us through the windows.

"Chase!" I yell.

"Yeah, man. We've got you covered the rest of the way. Door's on the south side."

Chase is waiting for us on the porch. Butch and I follow him in. The rest of the team stays outside to secure the perimeter.

"Where's Millie?" Chase says as we walk in the door. There's another guy there who I immediately recognize from Millie's pictures. Seeing him—alive and standing five feet from me—takes my breath away for a second. He still has the bushy dark auburn hair and spiky beard, but the gentle eyes Millie described are hard and cold and staring right at me.

"We lost her in the hotel," I manage to get out. "She left with her aunt. They're headed this way."

"You lost her?" Millie's dad walks up and pushes me on the chest. Probably not the best way to meet your girlfriend's dad. "How'd you lose her? You new to this job or something?"

Chase steps between us. "Mason. This is Millie's dad, Mack. Mack. This is Millie's boyfriend, Mason."

"Her what?" Mack says. "Her fucking boyfriend's in charge of this mission? Who made that idiot call?"

I push Chase out of the way and shove my finger in Mack's face. "Man, fuck you. How about the guy who abandoned his daughter for nine years doesn't get to have an opinion?"

He gives me a hard right cross to the jaw. He's at least a decade older than me, a few inches shorter, and twenty pounds lighter, but he still manages to spin my head around.

"What did you say to me?" He gets within an inch of my face. I've always heard he was tough, but his bravado is unreal. If I didn't hate him so much right now, I'd be impressed.

Chase wedges himself between us. "For reasons I truly cannot understand right now, Millie loves both of you, so why don't we make sure you both get home in one piece?"

Chase pushes me back. I'm in full body armor with multiple weapons and explosives hanging from me, and he still seems to think I'm the lesser threat. Honestly, I don't think he's wrong.

"Have you tracked her phone?" Chase asks me.

I pull it out of my vest and hold it up. "She left me a message that she was coming here—Azayiz's family house in the Birir Valley. Is this it?"

We both look at Mack. His face changes from deadly to just really pissed off.

"Their family house is about a half mile southeast of here. No one lives there that I'm aware of," Mack says, his eyes still firmly on me.

Just as I'm about to send a few guys down there to check it out, we hear an explosion of rifle fire in the distance.

"Hawk, where's it coming from?" I look over to him standing on the porch.

He turns around and grimaces. "Best I can tell, that's coming from about a half mile southeast of here."

"Fuck." I lower my microphone.

"We haven't gotten any signal here," Chase says quickly.

"I'm guessing I have stronger equipment than your cellphone," I say, shaking my head. "Base, this is Echo One. We're hearing gunfire about a half mile southeast of our position. What do you see?"

224

"Echo One. This is Base," I hear in my earpiece. "The image isn't crystal clear, but we're seeing what looks like about a dozen fighting-age males. Looks like they're armed primarily with rifles. They're shooting in the direction of a car. Looks like one person down and two returning fire. One is small. Could be female."

"Roger that. We think it could be our female target and MIA agent. Headed that way."

Mack's shaking his head at me. His expression is back to deadly. "If she dies, I will fucking kill you."

I decide not to tell him about the one body down already. "She's here to find you, chief," I say, pointing in the direction of the gunfire. "This is all on you."

"How about both of you shut the fuck up and we go get her?" Chase says, moving to the door. I pull him back and shove him toward Mack.

I look at my team and point in the direction of the gunfire. As we head out the door, I turn around to look at Chase and Mack. "You're not going anywhere. Stay here." I look right at Mack. "If you die again, she'll kill herself. I'm serious. She won't be able to deal with it. Stay here and stay the fuck alive."

We make it about a quarter mile when we see the car with a body—thankfully too large to be Millie's—lying near the front. I finally see Millie—in the same clothes she was wearing when I last saw her—crouched behind the rear tire. She pops up and gets two rounds off toward the three guys closing in on her. One of the guys falls. There's a man next to her, firing a pistol very poorly. He hasn't hit anything. My team scatters out behind the houses and walls above their position. I can see about ten other fighters still alive and slowly closing in on them.

"Millie! Get down!" I shout. She lifts her head just enough to see our rifle barrels pointing over the wall. She curls her body up into a ball behind the tire as we start firing. Fortunately, the guys approaching her don't see us quickly enough to take much cover. We have eight of them down within seconds. JJ fans out to the left as we provide cover fire. He has both of the others down within a minute. We stop firing and it gets quiet.

"Millie!" I yell. "Don't move. Hold your position."

I motion my guys out to the flanks. They slowly form a wide circle around her to make sure we're clear. Bryce and I make a straight path to her—guns high and ready to return fire. We make it to her without receiving any more incoming fire.

"You okay?" I say, sliding down on my knees next to her. I examine her to make sure she's not hurt. I can't find any bullet holes.

"They shot my aunt," she says, pointing toward the body on the ground. Her eyes start to water. "I think she's dead."

Bryce is already at the body. He checks for vitals and shakes his head at us. "She's gone," he says. Millie closes her eyes as a tear rolls down her cheek.

"Millie, we have to get you out of here. We have helos incoming in fifteen minutes. Let's get you safe until they get here."

She nods as she looks over to her aunt. She crawls over and touches Azayiz's face lightly with her hand. The rest of my team is back from clearing the area. They're all in a circle around Millie.

"Wait," she says, looking around quickly. "Where's Fareed?"

"Who?" I say.

"Fareed Custovic. He was just here with me returning fire. Is he down?"

The guys look around for another body near the car. There's no one. They all instinctively drop to a knee—facing out, rifles drawn.

"Base. This is Echo One. We've got a potential squirter. You see anyone on the run?" I say.

"Negative. Echo One. The only live bodies we see are yours and three headed your way from north of your position."

Butch looks up over my shoulder.

"Mase," he says, nodding his head up the hill.

I turn around to see Chase, Raine, and Mack—armed with rifles—walking toward us. I move in front of Millie and block her view temporarily.

"Keep your eyes peeled for Custovic," I say to my team. "He could have made it to one of these houses."

"You want us to clear them?" Hawk says.

"Negative. He's not our problem. We need to get to the evac site."

I pull Millie up off the ground, still shielding her from her dad. I get down on her eye level.

"Millie, look at me." She looks up, her eyes narrowing as she sees the concern on my face. "I just want you to know everything's going to be okay. Whatever happens next, you're going to be fine."

She nods and tries to smile. She looks confused. I kiss the top of her head before I step aside. She looks up the hill. I can tell her eyes haven't focused on who they are yet. I look up the hill, too. I feel her body fall back against mine as they get closer. I'm about to start whispering to her when something catches the sunlight to the left of where Mack's walking. I see the barrel of a pistol pointed right at Mack. He's only ten feet away from us now. I throw Millie to Bryce and run toward Mack.

"Nooooooo!" I shout as Fareed Custovic stands up and fires.

I knock Mack out of the way as I feel the bullet enter my neck just above my body armor. As I fall to the ground, I hear Millie scream. She's on me almost instantly, collapsing down on my chest. I see Mack pulling her off me, just as I fade into blackness.

Chapter Thirty-Seven

MILLIE, JALALABAD, AFGHANISTAN, 2020

"Do you think I have to wear black to the funeral?" I'm going through the clothes the agency recovered from our hotel rooms in Islamabad. There's not much black.

"I don't think it really matters what you wear," Chase says as he walks over to hug me again.

When the helicopters evacuated us from Pakistan, they dropped us off at the base in Jalalabad for a debrief before they send us back home. I've been crying nonstop. Chase has been sleeping on the floor in my room.

"Will you go with me to the funeral?" I take a deep breath as I squeeze his hand to let him know I'm okay.

"Yes, I will. I'll do anything you ask me to do, but I think you should ask your dad to go with you. Have you talked to him?"

"I'm not ready yet, Chase."

"Stop punishing him. You know he went into hiding to protect you. He did what he thought was right."

"I'm not punishing him, but I have to do the best thing for me. I can't take any more pain right now," I say, pausing for a second. "Is he feeling better?"

"Yeah. He's still in the base hospital, but he'll probably get out today. It's just pneumonia. Apparently, he's had it for a while. You know, not a lot of good drugs in that valley. Once they put him on antibiotics, it started to clear. He's not contagious, if that's what you're worried about."

"That's not what I'm worried about."

"He said to tell you thank you for getting his passport reinstated. Neither one of us really knows how you did it. I thought for sure he would at least serve time for deserting. Do you want to fill me in?"

"No," I say, shaking my head. "I don't. I'm glad that part is over. I don't want to talk about it."

The truth is I made a deal with the agency. I have the tape of Alex confessing to giving up Azayiz. If anyone found out the head of the agency's Middle Eastern operations gave up its most valuable informant, the agency would never be able to recruit an informant again. Director Ward talked to the navy, and Dad's back in good standing. The official story is that he's been working undercover for the CIA in Pakistan. I'm not sure how many people will believe that, but that's the least of my worries right now.

"The agency searched my phone for a copy of a video," Chase says. "They didn't find it. It must have been something really good. What was it? Who'd you send it to?"

I avoid his stare by looking in the mirror. My red, swollen eyes look back at me. "They have my phone. They know I sent the video to two people. They found it on Raine's phone, but they can't figure out where else I sent it—and they never will. The recipient keeps the battery out of the phone and the phone locked in a bank vault. It's untraceable."

I look back at him. He's smiling at me. "That's the system Mariel and I used when I got into the SEALs. I'm glad to see she's still using it."

"I don't know what you're talking about."

"Okay," he says, laughing. "Just know my wife can't keep a personal secret for more than two seconds, but she will take professional secrets to the goddamn grave. You're safe."

I stare at him for a second and finally crack a little smile. "I'm going for a walk."

"You want company?"

"Not this time, but thank you."

As I close the door to the room, I hear Chase say, "Go see your dad, Millie."

As I walk out of the housing area, I decide to head toward the hospital.

"Hi, I'm Millie Marsh," I say to the doctor standing outside his room.

"I know who you are," she says. "He's sleeping."

"I can come back later."

She puts up her hand. "No, not a chance. He would kill me if he found out I shooed you away. Like I think he would literally kill me."

"I'll try to be quiet," I whisper as I walk into the room.

His eyes are closed. It looks like he's sleeping. I tiptoe to the couch.

"When have you ever been able to sneak into a room without waking me up?" he says.

I freeze like a burglar caught sneaking into a house.

"One of these days it will work, Mason," I say as I slowly turn around.

He smiles at me. "Never going to happen. Come here."

I crawl into bed with him like I've done every possible second of every day since we got here. He holds up the covers so I can crawl under. He wraps his arms around me as I rest my head on his chest. After enduring twenty-four hours of not knowing if he would live, I like to hear his heart beat as much as I can.

"How are you feeling?"

"I feel great," he says, kissing the top of my head. "I wish they'd let me leave."

"Mason, you were unconscious for almost a full day. You lost a lot of blood. You have to be patient."

"Well, you know patience is one of my many virtues," he says, sighing. "It's probably one of my best."

"Yep. Right after modesty."

He grabs me under the arms and pulls me up to kiss him.

"Stop! You're not supposed to use your left arm," I protest.

"Stop being my nurse. I'm fine."

He kisses me deeply. I start kissing down his neck until I get to his wound. A round hit him right on top of his body armor. Luckily it hit him in a fleshy area above the clavicle, where there are no major arteries. It probably would have hit Dad in his head if Mason hadn't jumped in front of him. I put my hand lightly on his bandages.

"It's fine, baby," he whispers as he pulls me back to the other side of his chest. "I'm not going anywhere."

"If you ever jump in front of another bullet, I will kill you myself."

"Noted," he says, stroking my hair. "Are you still going to your aunt's funeral?"

"Yeah, I asked Chase to go with me. He said he would, but he thinks I should ask Dad to go."

"Have you talked to your dad yet?"

"No."

"Mills," he says gently. "C'mon, babe. You need to talk to him."

"It's cute you think someone who jumps in front of bullets gets to question my judgment," I say, snuggling deeper onto his chest.

He pulls me closer and kisses the top of my head again. "How long are you going to use that against me?"

"You jumped in front of a bullet. I get to use that for the rest of our lives."

"I did it because I knew you couldn't survive watching him die. After all those years—the nightmares. No way you would have survived that."

"I wouldn't have survived you dying, either."

He hugs me tighter. "I didn't die. Somehow we're all fine. Please go talk to him."

"Can we please quit talking about it? This is the only place I've been able to get any sleep since we got here. Can we take a nap?"

"Yeah, babe. You know that's allowed in the bubble."

I giggle as he pulls the blankets tighter around me.

Chapter Thirty-Eight

After Millie left me a few hours ago, my doctor came in and did every test in the book on me. She can't believe how quickly I've recovered. I think she's kind of pissed about it, actually. I nagged her for a few minutes before she finally agreed to discharge me early. I text Chase to see where Millie's room is and to make sure he's not there when I arrive. I knock on her door.

"What are you doing here?" she says, throwing herself into my outstretched arms.

I squeeze her tighter than I ever have, bury my face in her hair, and take a deep breath. She tries to pull back, but I won't let her.

"Mason," she asks against my chest, "did you break out of the hospital?"

"Yes, and I left a wake of destruction in my path. Anything to get to you."

"Mason."

"I didn't break out." I say, laughing. "They discharged me a few minutes ago."

I lean down and kiss her softly. The minute she starts sliding her hands up my chest, my lower body springs to life. I push her into the room and kick the door closed with my foot. I back her up until she's pressed against the wall.

"Mason." She pulls back a little. "Are you sure this is okay?"

"I promise you're not taking advantage of me," I say as I pull her T-shirt over her head. "Just be gentle."

"Mason." She pushes at my chest. "I'm being serious. Do you have permission from your doctor to do this?"

I run my hands down her shoulders—sliding her bra straps down. I gently cradle her breasts in my hands as my thumbs start rubbing her nipples. She makes a little sound as she starts to squirm.

"My doctor said I'm fully cleared for all physical duties I might have to perform. I think she was specifically talking about military duties, but I know she would agree this is much more important." I take a step back and pull my T-shirt over my head. I unbuckle my pants and let them drop to the ground.

She looks down at me—fully erect and pointing right at her. She smiles up at me. "Well, if the doctors gave you permission . . ."

"Babe. Really. If you can sex me to death, I'm willing to die." I take her by the hand and lead her over to the bed. "Come here," I say, pulling her down on top of me.

It's well after midnight, and neither of us can sleep. We've been talking and making out for hours.

"I think I remember seeing your dad pull you off me just before I blacked out," I say, squinting to try to help bring that picture back to my mind. "Didn't you guys talk in the helo on the way over here?"

"Oh yeah. We had a great conversation while I watched my boyfriend almost bleed out two feet away from me."

"I didn't almost bleed out. I'm sure Ty had a bag hooked up to me before we even made it to the evac site."

"Yeah. By the way, who knew y'all carried bags of blood on you?"

"Well I did, for one," I say, laughing. "And we don't all carry them—only the medics."

"Is that why you felt it was a good idea to jump in front of a bullet?"

"Baby, enough," I say, rubbing her back. "So what happened when we landed here? Did you not talk to him at all?"

"I really don't remember anything that happened after you got shot until I was sitting by your bed in recovery."

"Okay," I say softly. I know she's not telling me the truth, but I'm sensing it wasn't her finest hour. I'm going to let her keep that one to herself.

Her tears start coming again. I reach down to wipe them away.

"I seriously can't believe I have any tears left in my body after the last week," she whispers. "I'm so mad at him."

"Then be mad at him. You have every right to be. But you

do need to talk to him. Not for him. For yourself. It's the only way you're going to get any peace."

She nods against my chest.

"Don't ever leave me, okay?" she says, burrowing deeper into my body.

"I will never leave you, babe. Never."

Chapter Thirty-Nine

MILLIE, JALALABAD, AFGHANISTAN, 2020

"Dad? Where are you?"

We landed in San Diego a few hours ago, and we've already looked at three houses. We're on our fourth house now —a cute little bungalow near Pacific Beach. We're moving here soon, and Dad told me I get to choose the house. I'm standing in the street looking at the front. Dad disappeared inside somewhere.

"Millie. I'm here, sweetie. I'm inside. Come and find me."

I look down at my feet as they start moving toward the house. Wait. This isn't right. Why are they moving? I thought they were stuck.

I walk carefully into the house and see Dad standing in the kitchen.

"Hey, sweetie. This house is kind of beaten up, but I think we can make it work. I'll fix it up. What do you think?"

I duck my head down and wait for the house to explode. Nothing happens.

Dad laughs. "What are you doing?"

"I'm waiting for the house to blow up."

"What?" He laughs again as he comes over to hug me. "Why would the house blow up? You're really going to have to stop watching those scary movies at night."

I start patting my hands on his chest to make sure he's real. He seems to be.

"Mills, what are you doing?"

"Making sure you're real." I reach out and touch his cheek.

"Sweetie, you need to get some sleep."

Dad walks over to the table in the kitchen. He pulls out a chair and nods toward it.

"Why don't you come and talk to me? C'mon. Sit down. We'll talk about this."

I jolt awake and immediately look for Dad. He's not here. I'm in bed with Mason. We were up past one in the morning talking. I check my phone. It's only four, but I know I'm not going to be able to sleep again.

I take a deep breath as I stare at the wall. I need to talk to Dad today. It's time. I'm not sure if I'm ready, but I don't think I'll ever be a hundred percent ready. I'm nervous. I don't know how I feel. It changes every minute. I don't know what to say to him.

Of course I'm breathtakingly happy he's alive, but I'm also still in a little bit of shock about it. I'm mad. I'm confused. And most of all, I'm scared. I'm scared if I acknowledge he's really back, I'll turn around and he'll be

gone again. I haven't let myself be vulnerable since he died—
or I guess now that's changed to since he disappeared. I still
can't think of it that way.

I know talking to him is the only way to move on with
whatever this is going to be. I'm still not sure what I want it to
be. Does he think he's just going to walk back into my life and
everything continues as normal? I know deep down that's
what I want, and it pisses me off. I can't let him off that easily,
but every part of me wants to do just that.

I cringe when I think about how I treated Dad after Mason
got shot. I told Mason I didn't remember what happened, but I
remember it all. I remember Dad carrying me to the helicopter
because I couldn't walk. I remember him hugging me tightly
to his chest and telling me over and over everything thing was
going to be okay. I remember Ty trying to stop the bleeding
from Mason's neck. I remember landing in Jalalabad and the
MPs pulling Dad off the helicopter. I remember watching them
pull him in one direction and the medics taking Mason in the
other. I remember Chase telling me he would go with Dad. I
remember him telling Butch and Hawk to take me to the
hospital. I remember Dad saying, "I love you, Millie," as the
MPs pulled him away. I remember purposely not saying it
back as I stared at him. I was intentionally trying to punish
him. I didn't try to help him, to hug him, to tell him I loved
him. I just stared defiantly at him. The way I acted embar-
rasses me. It horrifies me.

Chase and Mason—and even Raine—have been telling me
Dad did what he thought was the right thing to protect me.
They all understand what he did way more than I do. I'm not
mad at them for thinking that. They can't understand how I

feel. No one can. Except Dad. I know he understands. It sucks when you can't talk to the only person who truly understands you. He understands me down deep to my core. I wonder what advice he'd give me about forgiving him. Actually, I know he'd be harder on himself than anyone else because he understands us—what we were to each other. He was my world, and only he understands that fully.

Mason starts to move. I can tell he's trying to get up without waking me. That's usually a pretty easy thing to do. I guess it's time to start the day—the day I finally talk to Dad. I roll over and look at Mason.

"Hey. Did I wake you up?" he asks.

I smile at him. "No, I was already awake. I've been awake for a while."

Chapter Forty

My stomach's growling when I wake up. I gently unwrap my body from around Millie even though I know I could probably drop a bowling ball on her and she wouldn't wake up. She makes me jump a little when she rolls over.

"Hey. Did I wake you up?" I ask, surprised.

"No, I was already awake. I've been awake for a while."

"Did you have a nightmare? Why didn't you wake me up?"

"It wasn't really a nightmare. I don't know what it was."

"You want to talk about it?"

"Not really."

"You need to talk to him, Mills. You know you want to."

"Not yet."

My stomach growls loudly again. "Okay. That's your decision. Do you want to get breakfast with me?"

"I want to stay in a little longer. Will you bring me back something?"

"Sure, babe. The usual?" I lean down and kiss her softly.

"Yes, please," she says as she burrows back into the covers.

When I get to the cafeteria, Hawk waves at me from a table in the corner. We always try to sit together so no one else tries to talk to us. We're not a very social bunch. I'm headed over to him when I see Mack sitting at the table right in front of me.

"Where's my daughter?" he says, looking up at me briefly between bites of his breakfast.

"She's sleeping in," I say. And then decide to add, "At least that's what she told me when she texted me this morning from her room."

He rolls his eyes, looking down at his eggs. "Well at least I know you'll never get away with cheating on her because you're a bad fucking liar."

"I would never cheat on your daughter," I say quickly.

He stares at me and shakes his head. "Good to know."

I stand there with my tray, not knowing if I should sit down or continue on to Hawk's table. Mack motions for me to sit down. From the look on his face, I'm thinking hiding in a corner might be a better option, but I sit down anyway.

"Man, I'm sorry. I know this is weird," I say awkwardly, and then quickly add, "Mr. Marsh. Sir."

He looks at me again, but doesn't say anything. We sit quietly for a few minutes—both acting like we're totally engaged in eating our breakfasts.

Without looking up, he finally says, "Chase told me you take good care of her. Thanks for that."

"Yeah, I try to when she lets me. She's pretty independent. She always been that way?"

"Yep. Independent and bossy." He laughs and sits back in his chair. "When I was bringing her home from Bosnia, we had a layover in Germany. I bought one of those baby back-pack carriers, so I could strap her to me. I fell asleep on the plane with her attached to my chest. I woke up with her hitting my face with her little hands and making very demanding noises. She was hungry and pissed I was sleeping and ignoring her. Her eyes were so intense."

"She still gets like that when she's hungry," I say, smiling. "Including the hitting."

He smiles for a second then looks down. "I feel like I don't even know her anymore."

"You know her. She's still the same person."

"You think she understands why I did it? Why I disappeared?"

"I don't think she's mad at you, if that's what you mean. Understanding it might take a little more time."

"I don't know what to say to make it better. She doesn't want to talk to me anyway."

"She wants to talk to you more than anything in the world. She's just being stubborn. She wants her dad. All these years, all she wanted was to have you back. Now that she has that, deep down I don't think she really cares how it happened," I say, pausing for a second. "I know you're having some doubts about your decision, but man, you did a lot right before that. She's seriously the best person I've ever met."

He stares at me for a minute before he replies. "She was

such a sweet, sunshiny kid. I hope she still has some of that. Her face looks so serious now."

"She hasn't changed that much. Underneath it all, she's still sweet, carefree, funny . . . This has all been a lot—for everyone. Give her time."

He nods and drains the last of his coffee.

"Sorry I came at you with the abandonment shit. I didn't mean it," I say, avoiding his stare.

"Yeah you did, but it's fine. You did a decent job getting us out of that situation."

"Yeah, and I took a bullet for you."

"Settle down. That bullet wasn't going anywhere near me. All you did was keep it from hitting the wall behind me."

"It would have hit you."

"Maybe." He shrugs. "Why'd you take it?"

"She couldn't have dealt with losing you again. Seriously. She would have died with you right there on the spot."

"From the way she screamed when you were hit, I don't think she could have taken you dying much better."

"She'd get over me dying—eventually. But she'd never get over you dying again."

He stares at me for a second and then nods. "If you think you taking a bullet for me is going to keep me from kicking your ass if you ever hurt her, you need to think again."

"I will never hurt your daughter," I say. "But you know my jaw—where you landed that right hook—hurts more than where I took the bullet. You've got some force there."

"You can never go wrong with a basic hook," he says, smiling. "You took it, though. Most guys can't stay standing if

I land it decently. You might not be as big of an asshole as I thought."

"Well, I wouldn't go that far. I'm definitely an asshole."

He laughs. "Chase told me once Millie was going to bring home a guy just like me. Looks like he wasn't too far off. I'm kind of an asshole, too. As long as you're an asshole for her and not to her, I guess I'm fine with it."

"Speaking of her, I told her I'd bring her breakfast. I better get going," I say, standing up.

"Let me guess: exactly three pancakes—extra fluffy—with strawberries and powdered sugar only—because syrup makes them less fluffy."

I smile imagining young Millie—blonde curls swinging back and forth—demanding that order. "Sorry. Now it's a hard-boiled egg, fruit cup, and extra coffee. Although the pancakes sound better to me."

"All grown up now . . ." He stares straight ahead at the wall. "Does she still like strawberry ice cream?"

"She never eats ice cream."

He looks at me with genuine shock on his face. "I can't believe that's true. Are we sure that's my daughter?"

"It's your daughter. She stopped doing things that reminded her of you. Now that you're back, I'm sure she'll be all about fluffy pancakes and strawberry ice cream." I smile. "I really need to get her the breakfast before she passes out from low-blood sugar. She has to be fed constantly. Was she like that when she was a kid?"

"It was like feeding a parking meter. I had to have snacks on me at all times. I'm glad to see at least one thing hasn't changed."

"A lot hasn't changed. She still surfs. And she's so much better than me. I don't even like going out with her. Maybe you can pick that back up again to save my ego from getting crushed any more than it already has."

He smiles and looks down. "I'd like that," he says as I start to walk away. "And you can call me Mack—for now."

When I open the door to Millie's room, she pounces at me to get the food. "Oh my God, thank you! I'm so hungry."

I smile as I watch her inhale the fruit. It's actually kind of nice to have someone to talk to that knows all about her very unique behaviors.

"I had breakfast with your dad."

She stops eating and looks up. "Really? How'd that go?"

"I think he hates me less now."

"He doesn't hate you."

"Millie," I say, raising my eyebrows.

She laughs. "Yeah. Raine told me your first words with him were—umm—challenging."

"We did not get off to a good start."

"He'll be fine."

"He's not going to be anywhere near fine until you talk to him. Are you done punishing him yet?"

"Just about," she says as she take a long sip of her coffee. "I'll find him after I finish this."

Chapter Forty-One

MILLIE, JALALABAD, AFGHANISTAN, 2020

Chase told me Dad was on the firing range. I head down there, still not sure if I'm ready to talk to him. When I turn the corner into the range, he's popping a spent mag out of his rifle. I stand there for a second, looking at him. He looks a little skinnier than I remember, but his arms are still huge. There's nothing I want more than to be wrapped up in them.

"You still practicing your shooting?" he asks without looking back at me.

The sound of his voice makes me jump. It's only been living in my head for the past nine years. Hearing it live almost takes my breath away.

"Not really. Just as much as the agency makes us to stay certified."

"Do they make you keep up your hand-to-hand combat skills, too?"

"A little." He still hasn't looked at me. "But after you died,

I didn't really like to do much of anything that we used to do together."

He fires a few more rounds down range—both in the target's head—just like he taught me.

"I know you hate me, Millie," he says as he puts his rifle down and finally turns around.

"I don't hate you."

"Well at least you're mad at me."

"I'm not even mad at you really. I know you did what you thought was right," I say, trying to mentally block the tears starting to form in my eyes. "I guess I just don't understand why you didn't take me with you. I would have gone into hiding with you."

"That wouldn't have been any kind of life for you, sweetie. I wanted to protect you from reality a little longer. I disappeared so you could keep living your life."

"You were my life," I say quietly. "When you disappeared, it disappeared, too."

As the tears start rolling down my cheeks, he walks carefully toward me. "Millie," he says, reaching one of his arms out.

I take a quick step back from him as I rub the tears off my face. "No," I say, shaking my head. "No."

He stops walking, but he's close enough now that I can get a good look at his face. His eyes are still so deep and gentle. They've always had a hypnotic effect on me. One look from them, and I always knew everything would be okay. I look away from them quickly.

"From what I saw the other day, you're still a pretty good

shot." I can tell he's trying to make small talk. It feels weird—like I'm talking to a stranger.

"That's the first time I've ever killed someone. It doesn't feel good."

"You were defending yourself. If you didn't kill them, you would be dead."

"That doesn't make it feel any better."

"I know," he says softly. "There's a reason I never wanted you in this life."

I look back at him. "I got into it to find out who Mom was. I wish you had just told me."

He nods. "I should have. It was a mistake."

"When we were driving to the valley, Aza told me a lot about Mom. It sounds like she was a force from the time she was a little girl." I laugh, remembering the stories, but then stop myself. I don't want to be happy right now.

"She was a force when I met her, for sure. She was every bit as strong as I am—probably stronger," he says, his voice cracking a bit. "That's true of her daughter, too."

"I wish I could have known her . . ." My voice trails off as the tears start to form again. This time I can't stop them. They start pouring down my face with the force of Niagara Falls. The second I look up at him, he's on me—his big arms wrapping me into a bear hug. I collapse on his chest—sobbing so hard that I start shaking uncontrollably.

He puts his arms under mine to hold me up and then wraps them so tightly around me that I can barely breathe. "Sweetie, I'm so sorry. I'm so sorry," he whispers over and over into my ear.

When I finally stop shaking, he guides my limp body over

to a wall and sits us both down against it. His arm goes around me as I rest my head on his shoulder. My mind flashes back to growing up in the Outer Banks. We spent so many hours sitting like this—me telling him all my childhood dramas. He rubbed my back as he listened and then always gave me the perfect advice. I've probably missed that most of all.

"Dad, I don't want to work for the agency anymore," I blurt out and then continue in rapid- fire succession. "And I don't know what I want to do with my life. And I love Mason, but I don't want to get married. And I'm not ready to have kids. And I don't want anyone to take away my independence, but I also want them to take care of me. And sometimes I feel like my head's going to explode because there's so much in there and it's all fighting with each other and I don't know what to do." I finally stop, take a deep breath, and look up at him.

His eyes are twinkling a little bit. "That's a lot, Mills," he says, grinning. "How about we work on all of that over the next few days? We'll work it out. Remember, I always told you that you have to do what feels right to you—not to me or anyone else. You never have to do anything you don't want to do. And that includes being with me. If you ever want me to leave you alone, I completely understand. I deserve that."

"I don't want you to leave me alone. It's not like it's all okay—because it's not, and I'm not sure when it's going to be —but I don't want you to leave me ever again."

"I will never leave you again, Millie. I swear. And I will do absolutely anything you want me to do. You get to make the decisions from this point forward."

"I want to go to Aza's funeral. She's going to be buried

next to her husband in Sarajevo. I only knew her a few hours, but she gave me my mom. All the stories she told me . . . it made Mom a real person to me."

"Are you sure you want to go back to Sarajevo? Chase told me everything that happened to you there."

"I'm sure. Will you come with me?"

"Yeah, sweetie. I will," he says, squeezing me tighter as he kisses my forehead.

"I want to see Mom's grave, too. And the place where you found me when I was a baby."

"Are you sure you want to see all that? You've been through so much."

"I want closure on that part of my life, and I think that's how I'm going to get it."

"I'll show you whatever you want to see if you think it will help."

"It will. And then I want to go home—to San Diego," I say, looking up at him. "Are you coming there with me?"

"Do you want me to live there?"

"Yeah, that was our plan, right?" I say, reaching for his hand. "We just added nine years to my countdown calendar."

"Yeah, Mills," he says, letting out a long sigh of relief. "That was our plan. How about we finally make it happen?"

Epilogue

Dad woke me up this morning to tell me he was going to the hotel restaurant to have breakfast. I almost had a panic attack. We've been in Sarajevo for two days, and I haven't let him leave my side. I still can't sleep. When I close my eyes, I think I'm going to wake up and he's going to be gone.

We're scheduled to stay a few more days here, but I think it might be time to go home. Maybe getting back to my routine will help calm my nerves a bit. In the last two days, we've gone to Aza's funeral, visited Mom's grave, and seen the building where Dad found me. I even showed him where Yusef and Fareed kidnapped me. I think I'm done with Sarajevo now.

When I walk into the restaurant, I see him sitting in the corner at the perfect table to have a complete, unobstructed view of everyone in the room. Mason always chooses that table, too. I guess some SEAL habits never die.

"Hey, I ordered my breakfast already," he says as he

motions the waitress back over. "Do you want a hard-boiled egg and fruit?"

"I'll have three pancakes," I say to the waitress in Bosnian. "With strawberries and powdered sugar on top—no syrup. And lots of coffee. Thank you."

As she turns away, I look back at Dad. He's shaking his head.

"I still can't believe you speak Bosnian," he says, smiling.

"Yeah. And Pashto. And Spanish. Some Farsi and Bari and a little bit of Urdu."

He looks at me, speechless with his eyes wide.

"I've acquired a lot of new skills since I was sixteen." I reach across the table to hold his hand.

"I see that," he says, squeezing my hand. "I feel like I don't even know you anymore."

"You know me," I smile as the waitress puts my plate in front of me.

He looks down at my plate and laughs. "Extra fluffy."

"It's the only way to eat pancakes. You know that."

"I definitely do."

"Hey, Dad, I know we have two more days scheduled here, but are you okay if we leave today? I think I'm done."

"Of course, honey. Back to San Diego?"

"No. Virginia Beach first. Mason's there for a few more weeks. And Chase is still there getting debriefed."

"Do you want me to change the plane tickets?"

"I already did. We leave in four hours."

"Still independent and bossy."

"You have no idea," I say, smiling at him as I stuff more pancakes into my mouth.

When we're done with breakfast, I call Mason to tell him we're coming home. I pack but decide to leave all the clothes Alex bought for me behind. I hope someone gets good use of them, but I never want to see them again.

Our cab driver is particularly chatty. I talk to him the entire way to the airport—in Bosnian—about his family. Every time I look at Dad, he's shaking his head and smiling at me. I'm not sure he knows how to deal with adult Millie yet, but I know he's so happy he gets to try to figure it out.

Dad's been lecturing me since we got to the airport about buying first-class tickets. As we walk into the plane, he looks around uncomfortably at the passengers sipping on cocktails and lounging back in their luxury seats. "Are you sure you can afford these first-class tickets?"

"They're on Camille. I told you how much money I got on her house sale," I say as I look for our seats. "The money's really yours. She would have left it to you if she knew you were alive."

"No, it's yours. I'm sorry you had to deal with finding your grandma dead. I should have been there for that . . ." His voice trails off for a second. "I should have been there for a lot of things. I'm sorry."

"You have to quit apologizing. I told you I'm not mad at you."

He nods as he grabs my roller bag and lifts it to the overhead storage. As Dad turns around, he sees the man across the aisle from us leering at me. He's been staring at me since we got on the plane. I notice he already has an impressive display of empty liquor bottles in front of him. He taps Dad on the leg.

"Damn, man," he slurs as he looks at me with disgustingly appreciative eyes. "You married up."

Dad instinctively steps in front of me to block his view. "She's my daughter, asshole. And keep looking at her if you want to lose your eyes."

The man's focus drops immediately to his phone. Dad stares at him for a second longer before he sits down next to me.

"Dad, I thought we agreed you didn't get to do stuff like that anymore. Remember? I'm an adult now."

"Did we? I'm getting older. My memory must be starting to fade."

"Dad."

"Millie," he says, taking my hand as he looks at me with his gentle eyes. "I know this is going to take time for you. I'm not expecting it to be the same as before, but I'm still your dad. I can't turn that off and I don't want to. I'm still going to protect you from assholes."

I take a deep breath. "Fine. But you need to lay off Mason. He's not an asshole."

"That's still being determined."

I roll my eyes as I reach down to my backpack. The plane is freezing. I put on my fuzzy socks and Mason's fleece and then cover myself with the blanket out of the seat pocket.

Dad grabs his blanket and puts it on top of mine. "I'm assuming you want my blanket, too?"

"Of course. It's good to know you haven't forgotten every-thing about me."

"I haven't forgotten anything about you," he says, taking off his jacket and wrapping it around my feet. "Including that you like a separate blanket wrapped around your feet because they get the coldest."

"Still true," I say, focusing my adoring eyes on him.

He smiles. "Why don't you try to get some sleep? You said you haven't slept really well in days."

"Yeah. Every time I close my eyes, I'm worried when I open them, you're going to be gone."

"I'm never going to be gone again, Mills," he says, kissing me on the forehead. "Close your eyes."

I take a deep breath and close my eyes as he starts quietly singing.

"'What'll you do when you get lonely . . .'"

My eyes snap open as I look up at him.

"What? You think I forgot your favorite lullaby?" he says, smiling. "Close your eyes, sweetie."

"'And nobody's waiting by your side? You've been runnin' and hidin' much too long. You know it's just your foolish pride. Layla . . .'"

Epilogue

When she comes into the bar, I'm sitting by the pool table in the exact place I was when she walked into my life a little less than a year ago. I remember when I saw her that time—it was like someone shined a flashlight right into my eyes. It's happening again. She finally sees me across the room and comes flying at me full speed.

She jumps up and wraps her arms and legs around me tightly. I close my eyes for a second and inhale the sweet smell of her hair. When I open my eyes, Mack's standing about ten feet from us, looking like he wants to try his right hook on me again.

"Your dad's staring at us," I whisper into Millie's ear.

She laughs, not loosening her grip on me at all. "Does that make you nervous?"

"A little bit."

"Well, I'm sure I can find another guy in the bar who's not intimidated by my dad," she coos as she brushes her cheek against mine. "I mean, Butch is looking pretty cute with his new haircut."

"I think I'm going to be fine," I say as I kiss her softly. "And please don't ever even joke about finding Butch attractive again."

She whispers in my ear, "Do you want to go out to your car for a second?"

"Yes, I do. And it's going to take more than a second."

I put her down and divert my eyes from Mack's as we walk past him.

"Where are you going?" Mack says to Millie.

"We're going outside for a second. I'll be back."

Mack grabs my arm and glares at me. "Hell no."

"What?" Millie looks at him innocently.

Mack keeps his eyes fixed on me. "You want to take my daughter outside for a second? Hell no."

"Dad," Millie says, rolling her eyes.

"What's happening here?" Chase says, spinning around on his bar stool.

"Mason wants to take my daughter outside to the parking lot," Mack says.

"Oh yeah," Chase says, looking at me. "That's not happening."

"No!" Mille says, pointing at him. "Dad's been gone nine years. You're on Team Millie now."

"I'm on Team Marsh, and I'm going to have to agree with the elder statesman on this one," Chase says, patting Mack's shoulder.

Millie walks over and stands right in front of Chase. "Yeah. You don't get to have an opinion on my sex life for reasons I'm sure you don't want Dad to hear about. Or would you like me to tell him about the shower incident?"

"What's this now?" Mack says, turning to Chase.

"Take a pass on this one, man. Trust me," Chase says, turning back away from us. "You're on your own, Mack. I'm out."

"Mills," I say, putting my arm around her, "let's hang out here for a while and then we can go to the hotel."

"Don't let him bully you," she says, looking at me. "I'm not sixteen anymore. I'm a grown woman. I can do what I want."

"I'm going to take the path of least resistance on this one," I say as I signal to Pete for a drink.

"Wise choice," Mack says, looking from me to Millie.

"I have to go to the restroom," she says, pointing at Mack. "But this isn't done."

"Love you, honey," he says, blowing her a kiss.

She scrunches up her face as she tries not to laugh. I don't think I've ever seen her look this happy. It seriously sends a warm feeling all the way through my body.

A few minutes later, I see Millie pulling a guy by his hand through the bar. I tap Mack and nod toward them. He hits Chase, and we all turn around on our bar stools as she pulls him forcefully up to us.

"Brian, this is my boyfriend, my dad, and my best friend," she says as she drops his hand.

Hawk and Butch come up and stand behind her.

"And I don't even know what they are," she says, waving her hands back at them.

"We're her backup singers," Butch says, putting his head

on her shoulder. "Millie and the Frogmen. Look for our new album to be released around the holidays."

She pushes Butch's face away and looks back at Brian. He's already starting to take a few steps back. "You have two choices," she says to him. "Quit harassing me or leave the bar with a few broken bones. What's it going to be?" She waves her hand toward us like she's offering him a choice of which door to open.

Brian does a quick sweep of the eyes that are now all fixed on him. "I think I'm going leave you alone now," he says as he turns around and walks away quickly.

"Good choice, Bri," Chase says at his retreating back. He turns to Mack. "Apparently, they're getting smarter."

"Unbelievably, it would seem so," Mack says as they turn back toward the bar.

I pull Millie between my legs. "So are you finally starting to embrace the protection of others?" I say, laughing.

"I'm accepting the inevitable. With Dad back, I can't fight the tidal wave anymore."

Butch walks up behind us. "Y'all want to play pool? Millie still owes me some money."

Mack turns around as Millie says, "Dad, this is Butch. He's on Mason's team."

"It's my pleasure, Mr. Marsh," Butch says as he reaches out to shake Mack's hand. "I know your daughter very well. Of course, not in the biblical sense like Mason does."

I shove him toward the pool table and start to follow him.

Millie grabs my arm. "Wait, aren't you going to be my partner?"

"Sorry, babe. Butch is my pool partner. You need to find someone else."

Butch turns around. "I'm willing to share, though—maybe a three-way?"

"Pass," Millie says quickly.

"I don't know, Mills," Butch says. "Watching you shoot that gun in Pakistan kind of turned me on. You want to go out sometime or something?"

"Are you going to stuff me in a duffel bag if I say no?" she whips back at him.

"You know, if that's what turns you on, we can talk about it." Butch laughs as he grabs his pool stick.

Mack has that deadly look again. I pat him on the shoulder. "Mack, if it were possible to shut Butch up, I would have done it years ago. Believe me, your daughter can more than handle herself with him."

Butch looks back. "Millie, who's your partner?"

Millie looks at Mack. "Are you any good at pool?"

"Are you?" He looks surprised.

"I told you, Dad. I've picked up a lot of new skills since you've been gone."

"Why doesn't that make me feel any better?" Mack slides off his bar stool and accepts a stick from Butch.

I hand Millie a stick. "Your dad breaks. I've seen what happens when you do. We're not falling for that hustle again."

She smiles innocently at me. "Aww. That's so sweet. Are you scared of me, babe?"

"Absolutely. I'm not even trying to hide it."

As Mack breaks, I pull Millie to me. "Are you happy, babe?"

"For the first time in a long time, I feel almost perfect."

"Almost? What's it going to take to get you all the way to perfect?"

She snakes her arm around my waist and whispers, "Maybe we can brainstorm ideas when we get back to the hotel tonight."

"Yeah, I'm sure we can think of something," I say as I pull her in for a kiss.

Read More of the Trilogy

Thank you for reading *The Only Reason*. If you have a second, please leave a review on Amazon.

What happens to Millie next? Buy the last book of The Trident Trilogy, *Wild Card*, on Amazon.

Synopsis - Wild Card

What happens if you find out the only thing you're sure about is a lie?

Through the crazy twists and turns of her young life, Millie's only been sure of one thing: her dad's undying love for her. So, what happens when she finds out he might not really be her dad?

There's another man who's been controlling Millie's destiny since before she was born—a man her mom married two days before she gave birth to Millie. Could this man be her biological father?

Once again, Millie must dive back into the fray to solve

the last mystery of her complicated history. With Mason glued to her side, she'll discover things she never wanted to know and walk headfirst into the most dangerous situation she's faced yet.

Millie's known from the beginning that finding out the truth could get her killed. This time she might be right.

Be social with me!
Instagram: @donnaschwartzeauthor
Facebook: @donnaschwartzeauthor
Twitter: @donnaschwartze

Visit donnaschwartze.com to sign up for my email list. Subscribers get first access to discounts, prizes, and sneak peeks into future books.

Made in the USA
Middletown, DE
13 July 2021

44124562R00163